Praise for:
Heart *of* Passion

Set locally at the Columbia River and the Kettle Falls, Peone's powerful descriptions of landscape and life cause the reader to experience the story in every way. One can feel the cold, the hard ground, the thrill and the agonies of horse racing, the fury of a poor loser. The tenderness between brother and sister, tension between father and daughter and the fierce bond between a girl and her horses are palpable. Characters wrestle with issues of willfulness, pride and desires for winning, ultimately learning some lessons about faith and forgiveness. Carmen Peone's own passion for horses and her spiritual beliefs give the story a strong authenticity; she truly has Indian culture and storytelling in her soul.

—Peggy Mandin
Kettle Falls Focus

Spupaleena, a daring young native girl, goes against the customs of her people. Instead of staying home in her father's pit house doing women's work, she challenges men in horse races, trusting in God to keep her safe while riding over hills and rough ground along the Columbia River.

—Ines Riley Helmstetter,
Author

Young people will find the heart and courage of Spupaleena as gripping as ever. *Heart of Passion* is a great story of faith and determination. The richness of culture and language, the strength of faith, and the girl who fights for her dreams…Peone fans will not be disappointed.

—Jim Boyd,
Singer/songwriter, Colville Tribal Member

A young girl with a love of riding and a passion for racing. Revenge, anger, guilt and jealousy. All these are ingredients for a novel of courage and determination. Spupaleena's dreams go against the "Indian way," the "women's way"—on the sidelines, watching. Girls just don't race horses, and they don't compete against men! But the strong-willed, faith-filled girl refuses to give in to family and friends' pressure, to risk and injury, to sabotage and fear of retaliation. She will race. And she WILL win.

Heart of Passion is the third in a series of family-oriented stories that show the author's love for horses, for the Indian culture, and for her God.

—Heidi M. Thomas,
Author, *Follow the Dream* and *Cowgirl Dreams*

I am honored to know Carmen and thank her for sharing her gift of writing, knowledge, courage and ever present love for God. She takes you through a series of passages which includes the culture and language of our reservation. While reading this book I feel a strong connection. This book will stay in my heart forever.

—Luana Boyd
Colville Business Council of the
Colville Confederated Tribes.

Heart
of
Passion

To Sally —
P. Round-Up

Heart *of* Passion

Carmen Peone

TATE PUBLISHING
AND ENTERPRISES, LLC

Heart of Passion
Copyright © 2013 by Carmen Peone All rights reserved.

No part of this publication may be reproduced, stored in a retrieval system or transmitted in any way by any means, electronic, mechanical, photocopy, recording or otherwise without the prior permission of the author except as provided by USA copyright law.

This novel is a work of fiction. Names, descriptions, entities, and incidents included in the story are products of the author's imagination. Any resemblance to actual persons, events, and entities is entirely coincidental.

The opinions expressed by the author are not necessarily those of Tate Publishing, LLC.

Published by Tate Publishing & Enterprises, LLC
127 E. Trade Center Terrace | Mustang, Oklahoma 73064 USA
1.888.361.9473 | www.tatepublishing.com

Tate Publishing is committed to excellence in the publishing industry. The company reflects the philosophy established by the founders, based on Psalm 68:11,
"The Lord gave the word and great was the company of those who published it."

Book design copyright © 2013 by Tate Publishing, LLC. All rights reserved.
Cover design by Ronnel Luspoc
Interior design by Joana Quilantang

Published in the United States of America

ISBN: 978-1-62510-561-5
1. Fiction / Native American & Aboriginal
2. Fiction / Historical
13.04.23

Other books by Carmen Peone:

Change of Heart
Heart of Courage

Dedication

To all my grandchildren, and any future little blessings God showers down on our family. For nothing is impossible with God. Luke 1:37

Acknowledgement

Thank you, Ashley Zacherle Caudell, for your wisdom in the world of horse racing as a Native American woman. You are an inspiration, strength, and vision for many up and coming female jockeys. Ashley is a three time Pendleton Round-up winner in Oregon for the Ladies Indian Relay horse race. She has won numerous flat-track races in northwest United States and Canada.

Thank you to my daughter-in-law, Tiffany, for all of your help with the missing Native words. You have a gift with the language.

Note From The Author

I would like to thank two individuals: JR Bluff, who is the Assistant Director of Culture for the Kalispel Tribe and oversees the language program, for assisting me with the correct pronunciation of the Kalispel People and cultural facts concerning their tribe and Marsha Wynecoop who is the Language Program Manager for the Spokane Tribe of Indians for her assistance with the correct pronunciation of the Spokane People.

Arrow Lakes Language Sound Guide

The **K̲** is a guttural K sound which is used deep in the throat.

The "**who**" is a soft blowing sound, not the word who.

The **huh** is a sound that comes from the back of the throat, as if one has something stuck in the back of the throat and is trying to get it out.

The **lth** sound is a lisping sound when the tongue is placed behind the front teeth and one blows softly.

The **ch** sound is a sharp ch not a soft ch sound.

The "**K**" with no bar is a soft k sound

Chapter 1

Northeast Washington Territory
March 14, 1856

"**Spupaleena** ("Rabbit"), the snow's not letting up." **Pekam's** ("Bobcat") coal black eyes grew wide as he swiped his moccasin covered foot across the ground. The buckskin-dressed boy shivered, shaking his head in concern. "The horses'll slip and slide. I can't believe this weather. It should be warm and sunny. The snow's already come and gone. This is nothing but clay…" He knelt down and grabbed a fist full of the slick, frosted mud. He stood and opened his hand, lifting the muddy ball up toward his sister in hopes she would agree to talk to someone in charge about halting the race.

Wind and snow attacked the terrain as it spun off the Columbia River, which was nestled in the base of the mountains. The frosted gusts surrounded the winter village of the Arrow Lakes–*Sinyekst*– people; its bitter fingers seemed to rob any speck of heat from their pit houses. Smoke from campfires hovered above the trees as villagers wrapped in elk robes scurried about, hunting for wood like scavengers looking for their next meal.

The sun normally shone on the Columbia River this time of year, thawing the remaining ice off the riverbanks. Not today. Mountains of pine and fir were washed in a blanket of white. This was the beginning of spring, the middle of March, and many of the women were preparing for the First Root ceremony by fasting and purifying themselves through sweating in a small lodge with woven tule-mats covering a willow frame. Spupaleena left that type of work to the other women. She was not interested in gathering roots of camas and bitterroot, although, she was afraid her father would force her to go.

Spupaleena squinted against the snow flurry, peering down at her younger brother as iced snow pelted her face. She huddled against the back of her leggy Paint stallion.

"What are you going to do?" Pekam said. He pulled his elk robe tighter around his shoulders.

A blue hand print on the left side of the boy's face began to run in a small stream, dripping onto his buckskin shirt. His horse had a matching print on his rump—that too began to run. Pekam wiped a stray hair away that was blocking his vision. Three Eagle feathers tied into the stallion's mane twisted wildly upside down in small circles as it whipped in the blustery weather.

The symbols were Spupaleena's creation, before she won the notorious race against **Hahoolawho** ("Rattlesnake"), her enemy—the fool. In fact, she created them just for that race as a symbol of honor and pride. She knew the male racers would have to take her seriously as a woman warrior dressed for battle.

"We'll be okay. Most of the course is on ground covered in grass, twigs, and rock." She nodded. "***Kewa*** ("Yes"), it won't be as slippery." She gave her brother a reassuring look.

Pekam dropped his gaze to the ground. He shook his head like a dog pulling out of his tether.

Spupaleena sat tall yet relaxed on Smoke'n Dust's back—Dusty as she liked to call him. She felt confident, ready to win, not caring what her male competitors thought of her—or her teammates. They had practiced long, grueling hours for months. They were prepared mentally and physically and more than willing to walk away with a win. Her stallion was just as prepared and fit with bulging, rock-hard muscles. He stood poised, ready for combat.

They were all one team in spirit and dress. Dusty was even decorated to match, adorned with three feathers tied to his mane with strips of buckskin. And on the off side of his neck, where no mane rested, revealed three purple crosses lined down the length of his neck in honor of the Creator. Spupaleena wore a tan, doeskin dress and leggings with purple beadwork tightly sewn on simply to catch the eye when horse and rider rushed in for an exchange.

Pekam gave his sister a sideways glance and scowled as he turned his attention toward the pain of his frozen fingers and toes. *This is going to be nothing but a slick, bloody wreck.*

"I don't know…" He jumped up and down attempting to warm the blood moving sluggishly through his veins. Looking around he saw some of the other teams arriving. Some trimmed in orange and others in brown. Then he saw it—the red circle outlining a dark, glowing eye. The fool had arrived.

Pekam gasped, jerking his head up to face his sister. She saw the crimson mark as well and smiled knowing her brother watched her every move. She wanted to assure him that everything works out to the glory of their Lord. The fool no longer troubled her as his horse now lived in her corral, breeding her mares. She grinned, recalling the sweet moment last summer when she beat him in the biggest race ever and won his horse. Spupaleena shifted her gaze from his horse to his face and the two locked eyes. His gaze was vengeful. Hers communicated the peace which surpasses all understanding. She no longer feared his evil ways, but instead meditated on the Creator's promise, knowing the truth: nothing is too big for him who has created everything.

Spupaleena grunted and looked down at her unnerved brother. "He's nothing **sintahoos** ("Brother"). Let's focus on our own exchanges today. We have to be solid on our feet." She saw the worry on his face. "Look at me."

Pekam tore his gaze off the fool and looked up at his sister, blinking away the soggy snowflakes clinging to his eyelashes.

"The Creator's in control. *He* is what gives us strength. Don't give it away to the fool. It's yours to keep not toss aside." Spupaleena spoke slowly, with purpose.

Pekam sighed and shrugged his shoulders. He smiled at his sister. "You're right. I won't give it away." He soaked in his sister's courage like the desert floor in a rain storm.

"Good. Now, let's get our teammates ready; you'll need all the time you can get to beat me!" A grin creased her face.

Pekam smiled, acting like he was going to pull his sister off her horse. They laughed, grew serious, and then said a quick prayer of safety and wisdom together before going their separate ways.

Spupaleena watched her brother scurry away. He was growing into a strong young man. He stood taller, was calmer than the past racing season. He actually began to think before he reacted—in most situations. Yes, he was turning into a fine young man. Even his midnight black hair was braided neatly, as was hers. At least it had been that morning. The wind pulled out loose strands, twirling them in its spinning current.

The snow continued to fall hard and fast. Horses blew hot, visible air out of their nostrils. They stomped and pawed barely able to settle their nerves.

Spupaleena sat on Dusty, focused ahead as she imagined a smooth run. She needed to look for her team's color: purple.

Five teams showed up for this new type of relay race, and each team had five members: one rider, two catchers, and two horse handlers for the two exchange locations, which were each one-half mile apart or more. Spupaleena scanned the area in search of her father and saw him nod, indicating her team members were in place. She would be looking for deep purple in a sheet of white.

"Purple, purple...I'm looking for you," she whispered, staring at the falling snowflakes in front of her. Spupaleena saw herself and Dusty jumping the first set of fallen logs. She would have to trust that Dusty knew the voice of his catchers when it was time to leap off him and jump onto the back of another waiting mount. The horses had heard their catcher's voice day after day for a year. She was counting on that and the white man's word, "whoa," for a nice smooth transition.

Pekam glanced back at his sister. *How can she be so relaxed?* he thought. He hopped up onto the back of his horse, gawking in all directions. He caught a seething glare from Hahoola<u>who</u>, whose long hair flowed behind him, plastered with white snowflakes. A shiver ran up Pekam's spine as he chastised himself for allowing the fool to get to him. He looked ahead into the curtain of snow and drew in a cold breath. He blew it out and sank into the back of his horse, trying his best to let his shoulders and arms hang loose. He asked God for the ability to focus in an attempt to relax his trembling body.

The racers waited for the start cry. The straggling onlookers remained quiet as they anticipated the launch of the race. They were bundled in elk robes and wore moccasins lined with cattail fluff. Their eyes were glued to the horses that danced and pawed at the thin start rope made from hemp. Shouts of encouragement could sometimes be heard above the rumbling of restless voices.

Pekam leaned down and pressed an assured hand against his horse's neck. He squinted his eyes, staring ahead with what he hoped looked like a rush of confidence across his face. It looked more like fright hidden behind frustration.

A whoop sounded in the distance.

A deer bound out of the brush, running for cover in the growing blizzard.

Horses pranced as riders attempted to steady them.

Spupaleena leaned forward. *Did I hear…?* she thought. She glanced around at the other confused riders. Then Hahoola<u>who</u> let out a cry, kicked his horse, and dashed off. In a flash, the others followed, their horses sliding on the slick clay the earth offered. The horses leaned forward, digging their hooves into the slippery ground. They fought to keep their balance, bumping into one another. Freezing wind and snow pelted the riders' faces, and their bright red fingers seemed frozen to the reins.

The sound of riders yelling at their mounts in the height of fear and frustration was overshadowed by a scattered trickle of followers as they quickly gathered closer, cheering on the team they favored.

Dusty's sure-footedness kicked in and they quickly caught up to Hahoola<u>who</u> and his colt. Spupaleena's eyes stung from the wet, hard snow pelting her with the force of a hurled stone. A blanket of white hid the trail they were traveling on—thankfully, it was only a half mile course between transitions. The riders focused all their energy on the shouts of the upcoming handlers in order to make their way.

Dusty and Spupaleena were coming up quickly to the first exchange. Her nerves raced, keeping pace with her stallion's pounding heartbeat. She imagined slowing her stallion down, jumping off as the handler moved into position to catch the animal bounding toward him, and swiftly hopping onto the back of the waiting horse held by its handler. The ideal transfer flashed in her thoughts, and she smiled to herself as her mind saw them tearing off for the second and final exchange. That image set her heart racing. If all goes well, it would be a liquid smooth transfer, one that would send chills down the crowds' spines.

"Where is he?" Spupaleena's voice cracked with alarm. She frantically searched the thick snow for any tinge of purple. "Come on…" She should have listened to her brother and fought to call the race off. It was too late now. She would have to toughen up and forge on. What else could she do?

Spupaleena was to the right of the fool and needed to get to the other side. Hahoola<u>who</u> glanced back just as she was making her move and he veered to the right, slamming his horse into hers. It was clear his intentions were purposed. The shady glint in his eye and the smirk on his face were the picture of a dark, evil figure. She had seen that image somewhere before.

Spupaleena screamed, peering into his twisted, disfigured face. A feeling of slow motion engulfed her as the pair spun around. She felt herself fly off, knowing she would hit the ground with a thud and more than likely slide to a stop, hopefully with no more than a few bruises. Trying to brace herself, she did her best to curl up into a ball, ready to hit hard and fast.

She heard Dusty scream as he went down.

Pekam and two other riders were close behind. Pekam saw the fool's vindictive move and tried to yell for his sister. It was too late. He saw Dusty lose his balance and slam to the ground, as did Hahoola<u>who</u>'s gray horse. Pekam and the others reined in their mounts, but it was to no avail. In an instant, the horses skidded across the slimy terrain, colliding into one another.

Pekam felt his bay stallion slip and slide and then all went silent.

Pandemonium broke out as a mesh of horse legs and human limbs tumbled and twirled down to the debris laden ground. Snow soaked leaves and needles entwined with twigs and mud sprayed in all directions. The sound of horse screams jolted the handlers of the waiting horses into action. They dropped the reins of the trembling mounts and sprinted to help their teammates, hollering over their shoulders for the next leg of horse handlers to come quickly as if they could hear through the dense barrier of the snow.

The remaining horses scattered. Most went only a few yards, turning in search of their handlers, while a couple of them ran as if a wolf was on their heels. They watched the commotion with wide, confused eyes. Snorting as their hot, visible breath erupted from their nostrils.

Skumhist ("Black Bear") knelt, watching the exchange from close by. As he witnessed his son, Pekam, slam into his sister's horse, his body clenched.

He felt like he couldn't breathe as panic entombed him while his mind reeled back a year to the incident of his son being dragged by a frightened, runaway horse. An image of his son's broken and torn body slammed his thoughts like a sudden crack of lightning.

Scrambling to his feet, Skumhist sprinted toward his son. He ran as fast as his fifty-year-old legs would take him, tearing his moccasins. His lungs burned with the intake of frosted air. His sides heaved and throbbed, and he nearly careened into the boy as he slid to a stop. Sweat ran down the sides of his face as if it were a blistering hot day.

Pekam was trapped and unconscious beneath his half-ton horse. Skumhist held his son's head, yelling for someone to come and help—crying out for God to help him. He shook with fear. He shook with rage. He hated himself for supporting his children's horse affairs. He should have listened to his gut and remained strong and disapproving. He frantically searched the crowd for his daughter, but failed to see her through the blinding snow.

Spupaleena stood, hunting and hollering for her brother. She caught a glimpse of her father hovering over a still form. Gasping, she hurriedly limped over, screaming his name. She dropped to the ground and knelt beside him. Blood dribbled down the side of her mud-caked face. Her head pounded as if someone had struck her with the blunt end of a hatchet.

"*Mistum* ("Father"), I—" Her body shook.

"This race should've been called off!" Skumhist snapped. He held his son's head in his hands. A mix of anger and worry crossed his face. He glared at his daughter—too angry to notice the gash on her forehead.

Guilt encompassed Spupaleena. Ignoring her father, she placed her hand on the horse's neck and rubbed him soothingly as the horse thrashed about. Spupaleena searched for the best way to pull her brother out from under him. No one was sure if the bay Tobiano had a broken limb or was just scared from having the wind knocked out of him. The white's of his eyes showed as he lifted his head and glanced at Spupaleena as if he were conveying his terror. She peered at her brother and fought back the tears.

They had to move fast in case there were severe injuries to the boy. Several of Skumhist's family members quickly made their way to Pekam's side. They surrounded the frantic horse, gently lifting him up enough to slide Pekam out. Spupaleena continued to hold the horse's head down, quietly singing to him, if nothing more than to calm her own nerves.

With one hand she skimmed clean snow off the surface of the earth and pressed it to her open wound knowing the blood needed to stop. She searched the area for a bandage hoping one would magically appear. She saw nothing. Riders never carried medical supplies. She grit her teeth, willing the pain away.

Koo_k_yuma In-tee-tee-_h_uh ("Little Salmon") had been holding his arms up in the air, ready to catch Dusty when he heard the loud thump of the horses colliding. The racers were still several yards away. He saw Hahoola_who_ ram his horse into Dusty, but that was not all he witnessed. He saw the evil tyrant pull a knife out of his moccasin and try to stick Spupaleena's stallion. Fortunately, he lost his balance and only stuck himself in the leg—a well deserved consequence.

After he got his wits about him, K̲oo̲k̲yuma In-tee-tee-h̲uh̲ ran as fast as he could to the wreckage. "Spupaleena, what can I do to help?" His eyes were round with fear and mud splashed his buckskin clothes and half-frozen flesh.

Spupaleena looked up with liquid-filled eyes. "Here, help me get **See̲ch̲ Sneewt** ("New Wind") up. He may have broken his leg. I'm not sure…" She glanced at her brother and saw that he was taken care of, so she decided to stay and help with the horses. She was sure their healer **Simillk̲ameen** ("Swan") would not let her in the tule-mat pit house anyhow, at least not until she had looked him over thoroughly. She was a short, stocky, stern old woman who barely smiled.

It didn't take long for the third legs of each team to hear the commotion and hop on the horses, speeding to the others, ready to assist in any way they could. The snowfall had not let up and it was nearly impossible to see. Hands were red and sore, bodies shivered from the cold and the shock of what they were seeing, and horses struggled to stand in the slimy clay underfoot. It was a sloppy mess to work in; nevertheless, horses and humans had to be taken care of.

"**Hun han neekun** ("Bug") and **Ta h̲uh̲t Skumhist** ("Sugar Bear") go find Dusty and help with any other horse in need." They nodded their heads and took off to round-up the strays.

Spupaleena glanced around, found her other teammate and motioned him over. Her body begged to shiver, but she shook off the fear and frost clawing at her. She had no time to fret as work clearly needed to be done. "***Chy chy pum Sn'e*** ("Screaming Elk") I need you to go get Pekam's horse and help me get him back to the corral. But first, have Pekam's teammates take back the other horses as well."

"Kewa, I'll build a fire and have my ***toom*** ("Mother") make us something hot to eat. We need to warm up." Chy chy pum Sn'e's teeth rattled as he spoke.

Spupaleena nodded, walking briskly to her stallion. The fringe on her dress swung back and forth as if being shook by a badger. She said a quick prayer for everyone as she went. She looked up to see Hahoolawho standing in her path. *God help me*, she prayed. He stepped aside and let her pass, but not without a bone chilling glare. Spupaleena glanced down and noticed blood running down his leg. She had no idea why, but decided it wasn't worth her worry. "I'm sure he got what he had coming to him," she mumbled.

Chapter 2

The following morning, the Sinyekst people were still on edge, especially the racers.

"I know what I saw!" Kookyuma In-tee-tee-huh tried to keep his voice low. He and Skumhist stood face-to-face in Skumhist's lodge. "He not only wants Spupaleena out of the race, he wants to hurt her. Seriously hurt her." The boy pounded his fist into his palm. "We have to do something. Now!"

Skumhist placed his hand on the boy's shoulder. Looking him in the eyes and talking in a controlled manner, he said, "Kewa, we will. I know you're telling the truth."

"*When* will we do something?" Kookyuma In-tee-tee-huh's eyes blazed with fury and his jaw clenched tight. He tore his shoulder from Skumhist's grip, not from disrespect, but frustration. His mind ran wild imagining what Hahoolawho was capable of doing. "The monster needs to be stopped. This was supposed to be about racing horses, not ruthless revenge."

Skumhist sat down on a tule-mat, crossing his legs, and took in a deep breath. He stared into the glowing fire for a few minutes until he knew the boy was ready to listen. "Soon, and you'll have to let me and some of the elders handle this. You focus on training for the next race—"

"***Loot!*** ("No") I'll help you." Skumhist softened his look, motioning for the boy to join him on a nearby mat. He knew how much his daughter's team cared for one another. They trained every day, allowing them to grow close.

The boy shook his head. Pacing allowed him to simmer the red hot fire steaming inside his mind. His braids were still damp and wisps of hair stuck out in all directions. His buckskin racing shirt was covered in mud as was every bare patch of skin—only a scarce amount of purple showed through.

Skumhist bit off a chunk of dried venison and began to chew, letting the juice slide down his throat. He glanced up at Kookyuma In-tee-tee-huh, who was now merely rocking from side to side with his arms folded in front of his chest.

"Please, just concentrate on training for now. I'll keep you up on our findings." The boy grunted, but nodded, respecting his elder. Not agreeing by any means, merely honoring the man.

"Will you tell Spupaleena?" The boy asked, raising his thick brows.

Skumhist nodded. "Kewa, I *will* inform my daughter."

"When?" The boy flung his arms forward in a questioning gesture and leaned forward.

"Soon." Skumhist watched the boy narrow his eyes. Kookyuma In-tee-tee-huh was clearly ready to protect his teammate at any and all costs, which warmed Skumhist's heart. "Trust me," he added.

K̲ook̲yuma In-tee-tee-h̲u̲h̲ grunted and scurried out of the six-foot, tule-pit dwelling.

Skumhist leaned toward the fire and tossed some twigs onto the dying coals in hopes of rekindling the flames. Sighing, he bowed his head to pray.

The tired, stiff father prayed for the healing of his son and protection of his daughter. He had made a promise to his family and God that he would support this racing lifestyle and was not about to back out now. He was getting too old and worn out to do much of the trapping he loved and lived for. Now he helped his strong-willed daughter and her horse endeavor. He would choose to honor his agreement—even when he didn't feel like it—which was at the moment.

Risks have always been a part of the racing world. Risks that cannot be determined, like weather conditions or another's harmful ways. Most people in the Sinyekst village believed that ill intentions, especially to harm another, were intolerable. Skumhist shook his head. *Why would he do this?* Skumhist thought. *Over losing a race? Losing a horse?* Skumhist just had no idea what the twisted boy was capable of. His daughter won the race fairly last year. It was Hahoola w̲h̲o̲ who suggested putting up the stallions for booty. Yes, he would deal with the fool, harshly and swiftly. God help him.

Following the wreck and after he decided to let Spupaleena walk past him, Hahoola<u>who</u> grabbed his horse's rein and jerked him off the ground and on his feet with a harsh word and a swift kick. The stallion groaned in pain and stood with a hind leg lifted up inches off the blood-stained snow. A three-inch cut ran down his nose and mud caked much of his gray legs and neck. He bared his teeth at his owner and shook his head so hard the metal in his mouth rattled.

"Come on you worthless beast," Hahoola<u>who</u> barked in his native tongue. The stud pulled back. His eyes were filled with terror. "Get over here!" The horse pawed the ground with such force, iced mud sprayed in all directions.

The stallion suddenly stood still. He seemed to gaze right into Hahoola<u>who</u>'s spirit knowing life for him would never be pleasant. The big gray sat back on his haunches, craned his neck to the right, and whipped the rein right out of his owner's half-frozen hands. Without a thought the stallion tore off, jumping over downed horses and humans.

Hahoola<u>who</u> watched him run off using only three legs. He glanced down at his rope-burned palms, spat in the snow, and kicked the ground. He clenched his teeth as a searing pain ran the length of his wounded leg. After catching his breath, he looked down to see the knife was still in his thigh. His blood-soaked leggings were beginning to freeze—as cold as his heart.

He wrapped his bright red hands over the bone handle and yanked the three-inch blade out of his flesh. Sticking himself only fueled the raging fire inside his bitter, ice-covered spirit.

"Are you okay?" **Ska ka ka** ("Chicken") took hold of his teammates shoulder.

Hahoolawho glared at him. "Get away from me!"

Ska ka ka's eyes traveled from the death grip his teammate's fingers had around the knife handle to his lip that curled like a snarling badger defending its den. "You're bleeding. You need help."

"No! I said leave me alone."

Ska ka ka took his broad hand away from his indignant teammate. He searched Hahoolawho's face as to why he was so angry. He had heard about the race his friend had lost to Spupaleena, but didn't know if that was really the reason he was so mad. Until now, Ska ka ka hadn't realized the extent of his fury. The tall, stocky boy was at a loss for words. After a short moment, he spoke again.

"Please, let me help you." His tone was firm. The rage is his friend's eyes spooked him. The hair on his neck rose and he trembled with uncertainty.

Hahoolawho shoved Ska ka ka backward. Grabbing his leg, he screeched, holding his breath. Heat rising from his neck and face matched the quill work on his shirt. He hollered again, not from agony, but from hate and frustration and the sting of his pride. How could this happen? He was supposed to stab Dusty. What went wrong? How could he have stabbed his own leg? Revenge to him was like air to his lungs. He had to have it. He would have it.

Spupaleena would not get the best of him.

"Get out of my way!"

Ska ka ka stood, stunned. He saw the stained knife in his friend's hand and the blood on his leggings. He gasped and his coal black eyes made perfectly round circles. He looked at his friend, staring at his twisted face. He saw an intense hate, one he'd never seen before. The red circle around his eye was smeared with his own blood and mud.

Suddenly a question that had pestered Ska ka ka came to light.

"Why did you pick the red circle around one eye as our team symbol?" He had to know the truth. He squared his shoulders and looked down into Hahoolawho's eyes, asking him to tell the truth, wondering if he could. Ska ka ka turned to face his friend directly and stood taller, waiting. Daring. He would not let Hahoolawho intimidate him.

A voice in the distance caught his attention.

"Hurry! Hahoolawho, come. It's your father. He's not well. Hurry!" **Toople,** ("Spider") another teammate, motioned him over. Worry crossed his face.

Hahoolawho glared at Ska ka ka, turned and limped away, clutching his thigh.

"Tell me the truth!" Ska ka ka watched his friend's back, waiting for him to turn and admit the truth.

Hahoolawho acted as if he heard nothing.

"You *will* tell me." Ska ka ka shook his head and went in search of his horse. His gut told him trouble had just begun. He was unsure of what his teammate was capable of. There were too many avoided questions and sneaky behaviors. They would have to talk later. He would approach the rest of the team and see what they knew. He was here to race, not be pulled into some kind of vindictive venture. He may have to look for another team to race with. Perhaps he would start his own.

Hahoola<u>who</u> stepped into his father's tent and let his eyes adjust to the darkness. Only a dim fire glowed in the center. His mother, **Impee-eels T-san** ("Happy Grasshopper") kneeled beside the ill man. Hahoola<u>who</u> crept up and knelt on the other side of him. The pain that ripped through his leg was temporarily forgotten.

"What happened?" He studied the uneasiness that covered his mother's face.

She shook her head. Tears slid down tan, hollow cheeks. "I don't know. He fell…just as the horses… and you…" She wiped the wetness of her face with the sleeve of her doeskin dress. "He said nothing; he just dropped." Impee-eels T-san's old and wrinkled face appeared tired. She held her husband's hand, rubbing it and talking softly to him in her native tongue.

Looking at the healer, who sat near **Quiy Ha-hau's** ("Black Crow's") head, Hahoola<u>who</u> gave him a questioning look.

The old and weathered man shook his head. "The spirits tell me nothing." Sadness in his eyes glinted in the light of the fire. He pulled an elk robe up and around his shoulders and began to sing a Native healing song. He prayed to his spirit helper for guidance. This was bad, dangerous medicine and the evil spirit causing harm to Quiy Ha-hau had to be put to death.

Impee-eels T-san scooted closer to the crackling fire, still holding her husband's limp hand.

Hahoola<u>who</u>'s anger started to boil, gaining force with every heated breath. "What do you mean you don't know? There has to be a reason. People just don't drop without any explanation." His voice grew louder toward the end and the red in his face deepened as he talked. He peered from his mother, to the healer, and back to his mother who was now rocking back and forth, seeming to babble mindlessly to the Creator.

Impee-eels T-san stopped rocking and leaned over her husband. She pressed her hand against Hahoola<u>who</u>'s arm. "My son, anger will not make him well. We don't always have the answer. You must go and sweat and ask the Creator for wisdom and healing." Her weary eyes begged him to leave. "We'll stay here with your father and pray."

She knew by the rage-filled look on his face, the boy was about to blow and that would be nothing but disastrous for everyone, especially her husband. Quiy Ha-hau's harshness with their son throughout the years tore at her heart, but she was sure he was only trying to make a man out of him. It was just his way. The old woman turned her attention back to her husband. She continued to rock and pray.

Hahoola<u>who</u> jerked his arm away, stood, and stormed out of the tent. He didn't have time to sweat or pray. A ceremonial cleansing would only be a waste of energy. He had no patience for his mother's weeping either. He hated how she defended his father. He was a cruel man and maybe this was the Creator's way of paying him back. The only time he had was for the sole purpose of getting that girl out of his way.

His mother watched his mud-soaked shirt disappear out the flap door. A tear slid down her cheek. Her son held the same anger inside of him as her husband had, but she needed Quiy Ha-hau to provide for them. He was all she had. Her family lived far away, too far; she hadn't seen them for years. Her heart emptied the day her husband took her from her family. They were young and full of adventure, which quickly faded. But now she was lonely and scared and needed them more than ever. Tears trickled down her face as she closed her eyes. She bowed her head, tucking her chin to her chest and held still, fighting back threatening sobs. They would, for now, have to stay hidden deep in her soul.

Hahoola<u>who</u> briskly walked toward the place where his horses were being doctored. His fist clenched tight, and his eyes burned with his own hidden tears.

"What has my father ever done for me? What has he done for my mother who has put up with his harsh hand and words for all these years? No, I have more important matters to tend to. They can pray. I will not!" Hahoola<u>who</u> went in search of his teammates to plan the next race…and an attack on the girl who tried to shame him.

Chapter 3

Spupaleena skipped her midday meal and went straight for her horse's corral. She opened the gate and closed it behind her, shifting in slow, careful movements, stiff from the previous day's accident. She made her way to Dusty's side and stroked his mud-caked hair. "I need to brush you down, don't I boy?" Her voice was soft and tender.

She stood by his right shoulder and leaned down, wincing at her soreness, to slowly pick up Dusty's front left hoof. She caringly asked him to pick up his leg and drew it backward, as if bowing, allowing him to rock his weight back and gently lay down in the bed of soft grass. The animal groaned as he placed his nose between his front legs and leaned toward his owner. She gently stepped sideways, whispering to him. With a quiet thud, he carefully laid his twelve hundred pound body on the cold ground under a brushy lean-to the teammates quickly built for him.

Since Hahoola<u>who</u>'s horse crashed into Dusty with the force of a charging moose, she was sure Dusty was bruised on his sides and shoulders. She would have to rub him down with soothing herbs. She ran her ice-cold fingers over his head and neck. The closeness to him made her feel warm and calm. She then inspected him for injuries. When her hand gently glided over his shoulder, he tried to lift his head and let out a heavy moan. She slid her hands down his left front leg, feeling the hot, swollen muscles.

Spupaleena took mental notes as she slowly examined his left side, the side the fool rammed into. Her hands were shaking as they glided over his trembling body and she felt her muscles tighten as her anger flared. She tried to ignore her anxious mind as it insisted on reliving the accident. She saw the wrath in his dark eyes—the fierceness in his face. With each thought she fumed a bit deeper. *Why?* she thought. Dusty whinnied as if to say everything would be all right. She glanced down at him and smiled, letting out the breath she caught herself holding. She leaned close to the black-and-white's neck. She felt the warmth of his body as she stroked his mane. She closed her eyes and sighed.

A tear trickled down her dirt-streaked face and dropped onto a white patch of hide under his chin. She sat up, wiped her eyes with the heel of her muddy hand and went back to her examination. She scooted sideways on her knees and took both of her hands and pressed somewhat firmly on his sides and back. Dusty kicked the air, attempting to run away from the pain.

A gasp escaped Spupaleena's lips as she jerked her hands off his body and hopped back. Her face scrunched with concern. She knew he was hurt, but had not realized that it was this bad.

"Did I hurt you, or just scare you, boy?" she whispered. Her voice quivered with grief. She leaned to the side and laid her hands back on his neck and rubbed him soothingly. She talked to him. She sang to him. She did whatever it took to calm his nerves—and hers for that matter.

She ran her long, slender fingers over his hide, trying to break clumps of mud off of him, singing a favorite traditional lullaby in her native tongue. "Baby girl, baby girl, what do you see? A red pony, a white pony, a brown pony. Kewa, three." Spupaleena gently rubbed his neck and legs in slow, soft circles. Her long black hair covered him like a warm blanket. She rubbed his body in rhythm to her songs. Dusty took a deep breath and his muscles began to relax as he exhaled and so did she.

The sound of footsteps came close. "What do you need?" Hun han neekun had been watching the pair from a distance for awhile now. She was touched by the love she saw from her friend to the animal she adored. Hun han neekun never realized a bond of horse and human could be so strong. She knelt beside her friend, placing a hand on Spupaleena's shoulder.

Spupaleena kept rubbing Dusty. She knew if she looked at Hun han neekun the dam would rupture. She had no time to feel sorry for herself. She knew God would take care of everything. He was always in control, no matter how grim things seemed.

"I need Honeysuckle, Nettle, Alder…and some bandages for his leg." Spupaleena tried to come off as strong and confident, but her friend knew better.

Hun han neekun knew her friend's heart—her passion for Dusty.

Hun han neekun nodded, still in her muddy buckskin dress and leggings beaded in the team's purple color. "I'll pray for him." Her small frame and delicate features conflicted with the warrior-like dedication to her teammate. Only her five-foot nine-inch height and sturdy determination held the second horse at the transfer site. By the looks of her, no one would ever suspect her post.

Spupaleena turned to the girl and smiled. "I'd like that." She instantly perked up, needing the encouraging gesture. The girls held hands as they prayed over the horse. He closed his eyes and relaxed even more, breathing steadily.

After Hun han neekun left to gather the herbs, Spupaleena noticed her stiffness growing worse in her tall, slender body. Her breathing grew heavy against the cold as the frigid weather crept into her bones. She glanced down at her soaked through garments. She would change into dry clothing after Dusty was taken care of. She chastised herself as that should have been done a day ago. She blew warm air into her fingers and rubbed her hands together. At least they had stayed a bit warmer from rubbing Dusty's fluffy hair. He had only just begun shedding his winter coat.

Worry burrowed into her chest. She prayed her brother would live. She prayed her father would not blame her, but she knew he would. Her body trembled and she glanced around wondering where the others might be.

Her teeth chattered and her muscles felt tight. "She'll be here soon." She rubbed Dusty with shaking hands. His eyes expressed thankfulness for her close touch. She tried to sing again to forget the bite of the freezing cold. Her voice quivered as the chill pressed in and her teeth continued to clank together, hoping they wouldn't chip. She coughed and wiped her runny nose on the back of her sleeve as she had nothing else.

Looking around, somewhat frantic, she caught a relative's eye. Her body now shook uncontrollably. He jogged over to her, touching her frigid skin. He turned without a single word and sprinted to fetch some help. Spupaleena could hear him hollering and it made her smile.

"Dust…I'm getting tired. I don't know why." Her belly rumbled and she grinned. "I guess I am a little hungry." Her words slurred and she struggled to get them out. She slumped over Dusty, taking in his body heat.

"Spupaleena…"

She heard the voice, but was too cold and tired to lift her eyelids to look at who those footsteps belonged to.

"Get some elk robes. Hurry!" he hollered.

She heard the scrambling of feet. She felt arms wrap around her midsection and ankles, lifting her up. She felt them carry her off.

"Dusty…" She was too weak to be heard. She didn't have the strength to see if someone was tending to him. Her body hung limp, too lifeless to fight them off and run to his side. She needed to wrap his leg and rub the herbal poultice into his hide. He needed her. "Dusty…" Did she even speak the words?

The Gardner's log cabin was small and modest, but homey. It was nestled at the base of a mountain, shaded from the heat of a summer's afternoon sun. Hand-sewn quilts covered the beds and separated the rooms, offering color to the dark brown space. Last year's dried wild flowers were strategically placed throughout their home. Herbs for cooking and for medicinal purposes were neatly stored in glass jars on wooden shelves in the kitchen, and a few leather pouches were tucked in at the end of those jars. A large rock fireplace warmed the rooms during the cold winter months.

Several years back, Phillip came home with one leg amputated leaving nothing but a stump after having a run in with some thugs. He and Jack Dalley had become partners in Jack's cow and horse business. He did miss trapping for furs to trade up river at the Kettle Falls, but loved working with the six-foot-two cowboy.

Elizabeth was thrilled to support her husband in a job that made him happy, and she was more than content with her fingers digging in the dirt tending her garden and raising her children.

Jack's place was a few miles east of the Gardner cabin. Both men ranged cattle in between and east of the two homesteads, and Jack managed the horses, that is when they weren't assisting Spupaleena with her colts. Jack gladly took the trapper under his wings, fashioning a saddle that would support the wooden leg. He continued to take care of his friend—and his family. It was the least he could do. The day Phillip left for Lincoln to fetch supplies was the day Jack would regret for the rest of his life. He should have known his cattle would care for themselves. He should have tagged along with Phillip. Then none of this would have happened.

Elizabeth Gardner held her year-old daughter on her hip as her two-year-old son clung to her leg whining, impatient for supper. She stirred a pan filled with fried cabbage, venison, and wild onion.

"Phillip, please come and get Delbert, I can't cook with him hangin' off my leg." Phillip Gardner was busy filling in the names of the racers his Native sister would be competing against this season. He wanted to make a chart of sorts in order to track her wins and losses. He and Jack were certain this would spur her on to win them all.

"I got 'im," Jack said, jumping out of his chair. He loved the Gardner children as if they were his own. His long legs moved quickly across the wooden floorboards, squeaking as he made his way.

Elizabeth chuckled at the site of the tall man leaning down to scoop her stocky toddler off his feet, and her leg.

"Is dinner done yet, Mama?" asked Hannah Gardner. She played by the popping fire with her wooden horse and doll, who sported buckskin clothes and tight braids just like her Auntie Spuppy wore. "It sure smells

Heart *of* Passion

good…" Her long, brown curls bounced in the firelight as she made galloping motions with the toy.

Elizabeth smiled at her daughter's hints of hunger. "Yes, honey, it is." She switched Lillian to the other hip and continued stirring their supper with a wooden spoon. "You must be hungry, huh?"

"Yep, I am. So is Leena."

"She is?"

"Yep, she loves your cabbage, Mama." She put the doll up to her ear. "She told me that her tummy is telling her she's ready to eat."

"Well, tell Leena that supper's nearly finished and she'll surely get a big plate since she is *so* starving."

Hannah giggled and whispered in her doll's ear. "She said to tell you good, and thank you."

Lillian let out a squeal and kicked her legs playfully as she watched her sister from her mother's hip.

Elizabeth held on tight so the little one wouldn't slip through her hold.

"What do you think so far, Jack?" Phillip turned the parchment toward the lantern so Jack could get a better look.

"I think she'll like it." He picked up the paper, holding it out of Delbert's pudgy reach.

> **Spupaleena's teammates**: Three feathers/three crosses—purple
> Ta <u>huh</u>t Skumhist – Sugarbear
> Hun han neekun – Bug
> <u>K</u>ookyuma In-tee-tee-<u>huh</u> – Small Salmon
> Chy chy pum Sn'e – Screaming Elk
> **Pekam's teammates**: Hand on rump—blue

Kookyuma Yaw Yat – Tiny but Strong
Quill Say Ups (Pia) – Red Tail Hawk
Kelowna – White Grizzly
Seelwha Sn'e – Big Elk
Hahoolawho's teammates: Circle around eye—red
Pelpalwheechula – Butterfly
Ska ka ka – Chicken
Swas Kee – Blue Jay
Toople – Spider

Jack chuckled. "Yeah, I think this'll do."

"I still have two more teams to add, but I need more names and translations from Spupaleena." Phillip rubbed ink off his fingers with an old tattered cloth. He tossed it on the table and took a swig of lukewarm coffee. He fingered the cup. "I think I need one more symbol as well…"

"She'll be here soon, or will you be going to the village?" Jack smiled as Delbert grabbed at his brown Stetson.

Jack snatched his hat out of the toddler's hands and tossed it onto the table. He then leaned back and stretched out his legs, accidently kicking Phillip's wooden leg, sending a sharp pain up his stump.

The tall cowboy jolted forward and frowned. "Sorry. You okay?" He grabbed hold of Delbert and straightened him up.

Phillip nodded, gritting his teeth and clutching his stump.

Jack gave his friend a sympathetic smile. He hoped Spupaleena would show up soon to divert his attention away from the clumsy incident. He sat still, staring at his coffee cup on the simple pine table.

"Can I get you anything?"

Phillip shook his head.

Elizabeth automatically poured steaming water into a tin cup with herbs to relieve pain and handed it to her husband. He smiled and nodded.

They were all a morning's ride south and across the Columbia River from Spupaleena's village, if one started out early. Neither the Gardners nor Jack had seen Spupaleena since fall.

"She had a race today, but said she'd head this way in a day or two. She wants to come and check on **Quiy Sk_e_t** ("Black Rain")."

Jack snapped out of his stupor and nodded. He sighed with disappointment. "Yeah, I hear Hahoola_who_'s still sore about losing him."

"Well, I bet he'll think before he puts such a fine stallion up for a wager again!" Phillip chuckled as he recalled the boy's sulking manner after the race. "It's definitely to Spupaleena's advantage. The beautiful red roan and his sturdy build will make for nice foals."

"Yeah, no wonder Spup calls him a fool."

The men laughed. Even Elizabeth smiled to herself—*a fool indeed*.

Delbert giggled just because the men did.

Hannah piped up, "Auntie Spuppy's the smart one."

Everyone turned and looked at her in disbelief. They glanced around at one another and burst out laughing, figuring she was deep in her world of make-believe.

Who would have thought the little girl had been listening the whole time?

Lillian squiggled out of her mother's grip and crawled over to Hannah, babbling a range of sounds.

Jack shuffled his gaze to his friend. "I just hope the race went okay with all of this unexpected snowfall. This is crazy for this time of year."

"That's all those kids need are more injuries," Elizabeth added.

"I was up early praying for them all this morning. I couldn't sleep nor shake a bad feeling hovering over me, so I got up and read my Bible." Phillip rubbed his forehead. He tried not to worry, but it was a struggle at times to trust God, especially when he so badly wanted to be there protecting her himself.

"Good idea. Never hurts to pray when our hearts are stirred up like a hornet's nest." Jack ruffled Delbert's hair.

A silence hung in the air until Elizabeth announced the meal was ready to be served.

Chapter 4

The snow had melted and the sun shone bright. The air smelled crisp and clean while a haze of steam rose off the Columbia River.

Even though it was warmer than the previous three days, the fire still felt nice and soothing, especially on Skumhist's worn out body. It felt good to be back in their home. Spupaleena finally had more strength after fainting and making the long journey back, even if it was on a travois.

"How's sintahoos this morning?" Spupaleena handed her father a steaming cup of tea and a bowl full of pancakes, which she had learned to cook from Elizabeth Gardner. It was her attempt to make peace with her father. She brought his plate to him, handing it over with a smile and a nod.

He grunted and took the food. "He's awake, but remembers nothing." The tone in Skumhist's voice made it clear his anger was still glowing. Spupaleena winced. She had feared the journey home would be too much for her brother, as he also was carried back by the jarring ride of a travois. She closed her eyes and saw his usual big smile and determined stance, allowing the corners of her mouth to turn up.

"Kewa, that's good he's awake." She took a bite of syrup soaked pancakes. Her body was still stiff and sore. She slowly and methodically rotated her head from side to side, trying to get the kinks out of her neck and shoulders.

Skumhist sneaked a peek at her, but said nothing. He was concerned about his daughter, but his disappointment in the race—no, the fear for his children's safety—overwhelmed him. His stomach felt like it was on fire. His heart was heavy. His appetite was fading. He had promised to support them, but regretted it deeply. Trapping was so much more fulfilling. No one got hurt. There was never a sense of panic, only a meal to eat and pelts to sell.

He supported his daughter when it came to breeding the beasts, but this racing seemed to be more than his frayed nerves could take. He needed to go and pray, asking God for direction and wisdom. There seemed to be little to no wisdom in racing, especially with this new style of relay racing. He saw nothing but danger.

Spupaleena stared at her father. "*Mistum* ("Father"), talk to me, please." She set her bowl down on the dirt-covered floor, seeing that her father was unwilling to talk, but she desperately needed to communicate. Her eyes pleaded with him. Her heart could no longer take the silence. She'd rather have him yell and scream, shaking his fist in the air. This stillness was suffocating like the dripping heat in a sweathouse.

A drum beat in the distance as a cousin sang for Pekam's healing on a nearby knoll. Spupaleena listened to the strength in his voice, closing her eyes and gently nodding her head to the beat. Her heart felt heavy. The emotion and sincerity in his voice sent shivers down her arms and across her neck. She shook them off. She didn't have time to blame herself. She didn't have the energy. Focusing on Pekam and his healing would be her priority.

Skumhist's long, grayish hair glistened in the morning light. It was yet to be braided. But his face and manner appeared old and frail. Spupaleena felt sadness for her father. She watched him struggle to support her and Pekam. Every time there was a mishap, he struggled to believe in them. She wouldn't race forever, but for now she needed his faith, his blessing.

"We'll talk another time. I must get ready and see about your sintahoos." Skumhist stared at the fire, swallowing his last bit of tea.

Spupaleena nodded as her eyes cast downward. She felt a heavy sadness cover her like the heaviness of many elk robes. A sideways glance caught him braiding his graying hair and then she heard his footsteps as he rushed out the tule-flap door. A single tear escaped down her cheek. She wiped it away and set her jaw—there was no room for pity.

Dusty needed to be rubbed down and his bandages changed, so Spupaleena set her empty wooden cup aside and rose. Feeling better, but still exhausted, she strolled toward the corral, praying for her father as she walked. Actually, it looked like her hands were doing most of the talking. She was in such deep conversation with God, she walked right by **Chy chy pum Sn'e** ("Screaming Elk"), who held out some herbs to her for Dusty. He shook his head and quietly followed behind.

Kelowna ("White Grizzly") watched the pair walking. He had been dressing some cuts Pekam's horse acquired in the pileup and now stood, watching the pair wander to wherever they were headed. "Spupaleena!" He hollered.

Spupaleena kept walking.

Kelowna shook his head. He finished the final wrap on the injured horse's leg and followed the girl and her shadow. The horse stood tied to the corral, cocking a hind leg. The animal was so bruised and beaten; he seemed to not care if he had to stand for awhile longer; at least he was resting. His legs were stiff and his sides sore.

Kelowna jogged a few strides to catch up. "Spupaleena." He tapped her arm.

Startled, she jerked back and looked at him with burning eyes and a raised fist. After realizing who it was, she laughed and her face turned pink. Chy chy pum Sn'e gave her a disconcerted laugh.

"Where did you two come from?" Spupaleena glanced about.

"You walked right by me"— he jerked his head over his shoulder—"as I held these out to you." Chy chy pum Sn'e shoved the herbs in her hands, smiling as his attention shifted to a friend moseying toward the river with fishing net in hand.

"Oh, **lim lumt** ("Thank you")…and sorry!"

"It's all right. **Wi** ("Goodbye")." Chy chy pum Sn'e took off after the boy.

"We won't be practicing for a few days," Spupaleena hollered after him.

Chy chy pum Sn'e waved to acknowledge her instruction. He was the same age as Spupaleena, but not as serious. He loved to be a part of the team, but never devoured it the way she had. Catching the horses was a thrill, but not what he wanted out of life and knew the job would be short lived.

Spupaleena turned to Kelowna. "What's up?"

"I came to see how Pekam is. Simillkameen won't let anyone see him. You know her…"

Spupaleena chuckled. "Kewa, I do. He's better. He's awake. Doesn't remember anything, but will be fine." She tried to remain hopeful.

"H-how's your father taking it?"

"Mad, he's really, really mad."

Kelowna rubbed his forehead. "I think he might be more scared than mad." He wanted to speak freely without upsetting her.

She stared at the boy beside her and saw the worry etched in his face. Her defenses dropped and her mood softened. "You're probably right. This isn't the first accident my sintahoos has been in."

"Nor yours."

"I know," she muttered. They stared at each other for a moment. Spupaleena didn't know whether to slug him or thank him for his concern. She could stand hearing the truth from her father, but no one else. It stung.

"Well—"

"I need to go check on Dusty, see you later." Spupaleena turned and strode off. She didn't feel like talking. What she really wanted to do was ride. Hard and fast. Away. Now.

"Wi." Kelowna watched her walk off. She confused him. One minute she was strong and confident. The next she was like a wilting flower.

Dusty nickered as he caught sight of his beloved owner. She rubbed his nose and slipped a carrot in his mouth. He chewed heartily, searching for more. Spupaleena opened the corral door and tied a rope halter on him.

"How're you doing this morning, boy, huh?" She rubbed his neck, letting the warmth of his body brighten her mood. "Let's check you out." She slid her hands down his legs and over his body. The herbs were helping, but he would need a few more days of rest before they could ride again. Then she would have to take it easy. These horses took a good spill, one she was in no hurry to repeat.

The ground would need to dry out and her head would need time to heal. She touched her tender forehead with the tips of her fingers and winced. Glancing at the sky, she was unsure how the weather would play out. Bending down, she scooped up a handful of soggy leaves. *Soon. We will ride. Soon.* She opened up her hand and let them fall to the ground.

"Spupaleena, come quick!" She jerked her head up and saw Ta <u>huh</u>t Skumhist running toward her.

"Where have you been?" She stopped in front of Spupaleena, sucking cold air into her lungs.

"Here, checking on Dusty. Why? What's going on?" Confusion swept over her face.

"It's your father. Hurry. Now!" Ta <u>h</u>u<u>h</u>t Skumhist clutched Spupaleena's shirt and pulled her forward. They took off running to her father's pit-house.

Spupaleena's heart sank. She feared the stress of this accident and the trauma to her brother had put their father over the edge. She slid to a stop at the entrance of the tule-mat hut. Simill<u>k</u>ameen held her hand out. The look on her face was stern. Her small, stout frame was intimidating, but Spupaleena was not afraid. She would go see her father and no one was going to stop her.

"Please, move. I'm going in." Spupaleena pursed her thin lips. She glared hard at the old woman.

"Loot!" The short, pudgy woman crossed her arms and shook her head.

Spupaleena had no intentions of disrespecting her elders, but…

Kelowna heard about Skumhist and quickly showed up, standing by Spupaleena's side. He looked at her, shifted his eyes to Simill<u>k</u>ameen, and back to Spupaleena's harsh but delicate face. He tried not to smile. The old woman was set in her ways and not about to be shoved around.

Chy chy pum Sn'e sauntered up behind Kelowna. He stood, smiling that ridiculous grin, peering at Spupaleena and the healer.

Simill<u>k</u>ameen glared at him, he smiled back, saying nothing.

"Move, Simill<u>k</u>ameen. I *am* going in to see my mistum."

"Loot." She shook her head, offering no explanation.

Spupaleena lifted a hand to remove the stubborn woman out of her way. Kelowna grabbed her wrist and pulled her off balance.

Ta <u>huht</u> Skumhist moved in between the two women. "Spupaleena, just wait. I don't think Simill<u>k</u>ameen's done. She was headed for some herbs when we showed up. Let her finish and then you can see him."

Spupaleena glared at her. She jerked free from Kelowna's grip and paced in front of the tule-mat door. "Fine, I'll wait. For now."

Simill<u>k</u>ameen nodded and went inside.

"I thought she needed more medicine?" Spupaleena snorted.

"She probably changed her mind knowing you wouldn't follow her directions," Kelowna replied.

Spupaleena grunted, continuing to pace. She hugged herself as if she was cold, but she was merely restraining herself from punching something, or someone. How dare that old woman keep her from comforting her father? She would have to speak with an elder or perhaps directly to the Salmon chief. The corners of her mouth turned up and a glint shown in her eyes.

The rest of Spupaleena's and Pekam's team members straggled up to the circle of friends and waited with her. They watched Spupaleena walk back and forth in front of the pit house like a sentry guarding a prisoner. No one knew the details of what happened or exactly why they were there by their friend's side. But when one was in trouble, they all came in droves to support the one they loved.

Spupaleena continued to pace. Kelowna sat down with his head resting on his hands. Chy chy pum Sn'e smiled, looking at everyone. The rest gathered pieces of wood to sit on while they waited. They waited in silence, listening to the drumbeat in the distance.

Hahoola<u>who</u> gathered his flock. It had been a week since the pileup. He paced with a hitch in his step, contemplating how he would approach the subject. A sudden sharp pain caused him to hunch over and grab his leg; the wound was a constant reminder of what his error had cost him. He let out a guttural growl and stood straight. His teammates glanced at one another with puzzled looks on their faces, wondering why they were in his pit-house. They were all just sitting down to eat dinner when they heard their fearless leader bellowing like a mad man, summoning them to his place.

They lived with their families in a small village north of the Kettle Falls fishing site on the Columbia River, north of Spupaleena's village. It had been a long two days catching their run-away horses and making their way home. After the disastrous race, and now, after a few days of rest, Hahoola<u>who</u> had plenty of time to fume. To plan. The boys sat exhausted and the girls twitched with irritation. Darkness had settled and only the light of the glowing fire lit the dwelling. The young racers sat on tule-mats around the fire, glancing at one another, faces flustered. What could be so important?

Toople lifted his hands angrily, jabbing the air. "What's this about?"

Hahoola<u>who</u> stopped, turned, and smiled. He ran his fingers down the smooth wood handle of the hatchet in his hand.

Ska ka ka rolled his eyes, shifting them to the fire. He was about sick of Hahoola<u>who</u>'s madness, acting like a lunatic. He rubbed his hands against the heat of the glowing embers.

Swas Kee ("Blue Jay") grinned, looking forward to what his idol had to say. He sat up straight with his eyes glued on his leader.

"We need to do whatever it takes to win the next race." Hahoola<u>who</u> talked slowly, as if the men were little children and he was the teacher.

"Just say what you mean." Toople was losing his patience as fast as a coyote pouncing on a fat, juicy quail.

Hahoola<u>who</u> glared at him, holding his hand out to stop his words. Toople gave him an impatient look. He leaned forward to rise, but stopped at Hahoola<u>who</u>'s words.

"I have a plan."

"Well, isn't that refreshing?" Toople said, dripping in sarcasm. He leaned back, curious to hear what the maniac had to say.

This time he was ignored.

"What is it?" Swas Kee asked, giving his wicked commander a huge grin. He leaned forward, ready to receive the cleverly warped instructions.

"We need to take out Spupaleena's horse. She can't win without him." He gazed into the fire, smiling, planning. He rubbed his hands together, happy with his decision. He stopped, continuing to twirl the hatchet around, "All of them…"

Ska ka ka sat stunned, staring at the purely malevolent man before him.

Toople smiled, methods of restraint reeling through that sick mind of his.

Pelpalweechula just shook her head in disbelief. Who cared about the girl and her horse?

Swas Kee's eyes danced with excitement as he clapped his hands.

"This is ridiculous! We just need to ride and not worry about what the competition is doing. Our horses are—"

"No. We're not worrying about the other teams," he quieted his voice, smiled, and continued. "I—we are merely ensuring our win. A win that we deserve." Hahoolawho cackled. "What we have worked so hard for, it's ours and *only* ours."

Pelpalweechula rolled her eyes. "I only care about riding. I'm not concerned about your sick affairs with the girl. I care about our team, our efforts, and yes—our win."

Ska ka ka nodded. "I won't be involved in your fight with Spupaleena either. I'll be a part of your team, but not your revenge. It's yours not mine. Do *not* put me in the middle of it." Ska ka ka got up and scurried out the tule-mat flap door. Pelpalweechula hurried to catch up. They had both had enough of his foolishness.

Toople glanced at Swas Kee and smiled. "We'll help you. It will be easy to replace those two. We can find riders that have talent and dedication." He jumped to his feet and stood near Hahoola<u>who</u>.

Swas Kee nodded enthusiastically, like a small child being asked if he wanted a treat.

Hahoola<u>who</u> looked deep in their eyes. He needed to be sure they would not back out. He never needed the others's approval and help, or so he thought. The three of them would succeed. He grinned, running his finger down the length of a scar that started at the top of his skull and ran to the top of his ear. *We will win.*

Chapter 5

The afternoon was warm and the sun shone brightly. Skumhist had fully recovered from the sensation that felt like his heart was burning, and the healer had instructed him to rest. She had given him some herbs to soothe his nerves. He took the time to walk in the woods and even set a few snares.

There was no fire needed in the pit-home; it had long died out. Pekam was nestled in his elk robe. With his sad looking eyes, he begged his sister to let him get up and ride. Three weeks had passed, and he still remembered nothing, but the pain in his body and head told him something bad had taken place.

"Is it true?" Pekam rubbed his head. He tried to sit up, but the pain slammed him back down to his grass-stuffed, buckskin pillow. "Did the fool try to stab you?"

Spupaleena shrugged. "I don't know. It may have been me he was after and it may have been Dusty." She lowered her gaze.

"**_Lthkickha_**" ("Older Sister"), tell me what happened the day of the race. Mistum won't tell me anything. I think he's afraid he'll upset me." Spupaleena shook her head and Pekam lowered his gaze. She clutched her braids and ran her hands half way down her waist-long hair. He was placing her in a tough spot.

Pekam had the right to know. He was young and spry, but perhaps he did need to take some time off. Maybe their father was right. Her heart told her to tell him the truth, but her ties to the people and their culture reminded her to respect her elders and do as she was asked.

Confusion engulfed her. How could she ever forgive herself if he wrecked and was once again hurt? She couldn't. *God, help me. What should I do? How should I handle this? I'm so mixed up. I feel like two dogs fighting inside of me. Help me Father. Please.*

Taking in a deep breath and then letting it slip between her lips, she finally spoke. "Sintahoos, I—"

"Wi, my *squasee* ("Son"). How are you feeling today?" Skumhist burst through the tule-mat door. He was smiling brightly, holding the rabbit he had just caught in one hand and a hunk of dried deer meat for Pekam in the other. Looking down, he saw his daughter sitting beside his wounded son. His smile faded. His bright sunny face instantly turned into a stormy night.

"Father, lthkickha and I were just talking." The tone of Pekam's voice quivered.

Skumhist tossed the dead varmint on the dirt floor in disgust. His gaze shifted toward his son. "About?"

The siblings peered at one another as if they had been caught in a lie.

Skumhist laid the meat down by his son.

Pekam looked at the freshly dried venison. His nostrils flared as he took in the aroma. His mouth watered. "For me?"

Skumhist slowly nodded. "Kewa." Your cousin made it just for you before he left to set some snares for dinner."

Pleasure crossed Pekam's face. How fun it would be to tromp in the woods. He sometimes missed those days with his father. Seeing the catch for the next meal was a mighty feeling, one of providing—of manhood. Whatever it was called, he bubbled with the thrill of adventure. He was sick of lying in bed. He was sick of the stuffy, smoke-filled air and sore ribs. He longed to ride and draw in a lung full of fresh, crisp air. He needed to feel the power of his horse underneath him; he longed for that surge of adrenalin that gave him a high in life like no other.

"Pekam…"

The boy looked at his father, who snatched him out of his daydreaming. Skumhist shook his head. "Kewa?"

"Mistum, I think…" Spupaleena trembled with anxiety. "I think we should tell him."

Skumhist tossed her the most piercing glare ever. She felt like maybe she needed to check herself for little pin-holes or burn marks on her skin and clothing. She wiped her sweat soaked hands on her leggings that rested underneath her doeskin dress. Most women only wore the dress with knee-high moccasins. Not Spupaleena. She wore the pants to protect her legs from brush and trees when riding. They served the same purpose as what her white friends called chaps. But then, most women did forgo racing horses.

Pekam stared at his father with pleading, round eyes. Those black eyes begged for the truth, and Skumhist was a man of integrity. He knew deep down that the truth sets people free and his son needed that freedom. Otherwise, it would hang over his shoulders, taunting him for life.

Skumhist's expression softened and he nodded. "We need to pray first." He knelt beside his son. All three joined hands as they prayed for forgiveness and wisdom. Then Skumhist and Spupaleena laid hands on Pekam and prayed for the boy's healing, as they had done separately every day since the accident.

"I would like to tell him about the wreck." Spupaleena spoke softly, looking at her father.

"Kewa." Skumhist nodded.

She turned to her brother, who had a look of peace, anticipation, and fright all mixed in one jumbled mess on his face. He nodded, with both eyebrows arched. She was taking too much time to gather her thoughts. *Just spill it*, he thought. How it came out never mattered, just that he heard it did.

"Do you remember getting ready?"

"Loot." He shook his head, grabbing it with both hands and wincing. He groaned.

Spupaleena's heart lurched. She hated to see her brother in so much pain. After a few seconds, she rubbed her hands together in her lap and began. "Do you remember telling me the ground was too slick to race? That you were worried?"

Skumhist gave her a questioning look.

"Loot." Pekam slowly shook his head; his hands still gripping the sides of it.

"Sintahoos, I first need to ask you to forgive me. I put you in harm's way. I should have cancelled the race, or fought to have it cancelled or pulled out…pulled you out."

"I forgive you. Now just tell me what happened. We have no way of controlling the weather you know." Pekam picked up a wooden cup of water and took a drink. He began to sweat and tremble, anticipating the story he was about to hear. The somber look on his sister's face and his impatience was no help.

Spupaleena gave him a small smile, remembering he was a jittery, teenage boy. She glanced at her father, who nodded, encouraging her to continue.

She told him about the wreck, assuring him the horses were all in good health, just banged up with minor cuts and bruises.

He looked at her forehead and saw the now healing purple scar his sister sported. "I see you're wearing your colors." He smiled brightly.

Spupaleena chuckled, bringing the tips of her fingers up to the gash above her brow. "Kewa. I suppose it's my battle scar."

"Kewa. A real warrior woman!" he teased. They looked at each other and giggled.

Skumhist frowned, shifting his weight and clearing his throat. He ran both hands down his braids and sighed heavily. He peered at his children and the look on his face spoke of his own frustration and need to be serious. The siblings peered at him and stopped snickering.

"Really sintahoos, you need to watch your head. No more accidents. Your brain could be hurt forever. Please, you need to—"

"Stop! I won't give up racing."

Skumhist glared at the boy. "Listen to your—"

"Mistum, loot. I know what you're going to say. I've thought a lot about this. I won't give up racing. I love it. I love riding. I love the horses. I will not stop. It makes me feel alive, like I'm worth something. I feel brave for once in my life. But..." he looked up and gave them a tantalizing smile, pleading with his eyes. "I will be careful. I won't take chances. Next time I'll pull out even if everyone else stays in the race." He looked at his father. "Mistum, it's in my blood like trapping was in yours. I know you miss it. I can see it in your eyes. I may be young, but I do notice the change in you. Please don't take it away from me." Pekam's gaze shifted to his sister. "Lthkickha, don't ask me to quit. I won't." Tears pooled in his eyes.

Spupaleena and Skumhist exchanged glances. They locked eyes briefly, knowing if they fought him he would take off and race anyway. Better to support him and make sure he trains properly than to leave him to his own demise.

Skumhist placed his strong, aging hand on his son's shoulder. "Kewa, I won't ask you to quit. But I will insist that you train with your sister and listen and obey her every word. She knows what she's doing—

most of the time." He gave his daughter a harsh glance, brows arched.

Pekam nodded, but not too hard, his head couldn't take the sharp pain. "Kewa, I will, mistum. I won't let you down. I promise."

Skumhist grunted. "Just let your yes be yes. Don't make promises you can't keep, Pekam. Just take our words seriously and show me with your actions that you are genuine, or you will be done."

"Kewa, I understand." Pekam was more than a little impatient with their drilling. He said he would be earnest and he meant it. Enough already.

Spupaleena stood. "I need to go check on Dusty, I'll check on See<u>ch</u> Sneewt as well."

"Lim lumt. I can't wait to see him."

Skumhist rubbed his chin and turned to his son. "Why *did* you name him New Wind?"

Pekam grinned, looking a bit sheepish. "Because, a New Wind is going to blow in and whip the others away in its twirling, twisting, powerful path." His eye's shone with excitement and he sat somewhat straighter.

Spupaleena laughed as she walked out the door. "Can't wait to see that!"

Skumhist chuckled. "Me either. Now get some more rest. I will have the healer come in and check on you later."

"You guys can laugh all you want, he's fast…faster than Dusty," Pekam said, raising his voice in hopes of having his sister's ears hear his promise. He caught his breath at the jabbing pain of his bruised ribs.

All he could hear were fading chuckles.

Pekam smiled. He knew his sister had a gigantic surprise coming her way.

"Spupaleena should have been here by now." Phillip paced with a limp as the creaky floor of his cabin groaned. His tattered shirt hung loose, and his work pants and boots were covered with mud. He ran both hands through his sandy blond hair. He had his walking stick in hand, ready to use it in more ways than just a walking aid. "It's been almost a month."

"Phillip…" Elizabeth stood, scowling with one hand on her broom and the other planted firmly on her hip. She watched her worried husband leave dirty footprints on her floor, the one she had just swept moments ago. Her floral apron hung neatly over her gingham dress. Her blond hair was tightly wrapped in a bun at the nape of her neck. She stood, tapping her foot, almost in time with Phillip's frantic steps.

"What. Where do you think she is? Is Skumhist okay, you know he hasn't been feeling the best. Did she get hurt? I think—"

"I think you need to quit frett'n and trust that the girl knows what she's doing."

Phillip stopped. "You know her, she's flighty. What if she got mad and took off again. She always—"

"Phillip, she always what? Is still a small child who lets her emotions rule over her? Huh? That she hasn't grown up? Quit treating her like a child. What has gotten into you? You don't fuss like this. That's my job." She winked at her husband.

Spupaleena was like a little sister to them both. No, more like a daughter. Phillip's mind seemed to linger in the past the last few days. He clearly saw the image of that blizzard swept afternoon he had discovered her body laying in the snow, broken and nearly dead. She was thirteen when Phillip had found her half frozen and barely breathing in a snow storm. He brought her from across the Columbia River to their cabin for his wife to heal. Spupaleena had stayed many months with them wherein they forged an unbreakable bond.

Spupaleena was now a young woman and it was a stretch for Phillip to see her in that light. He couldn't imagine the turmoil Skumhist felt in letting her grow up.

Phillip glanced at Hannah, lying peacefully in her bed. How would he ever let his spunky little daughter, his flesh and blood, do the same? He shuddered at the thought. He shook his head, halting his racing mind of the horrifying thoughts.

Elizabeth watched him study their daughter. "Yes, it will be hard to let her go, but it's destined to happen. Isn't that what parents do? Raise their children to succeed on their own? Fly the coop? Leave the nest? They always come back..." *Unless they move far away, like she did.* Her heart began to pound.

"You're right."

Elizabeth gasped. She wiped the sweat from her brow. *Oh, Lord. Prepare us for that day. Please start now.*

Without thought she started to sweep, humming to chase away her worry. She liked to hum; it soothed her nerves, calming her so she could think. Think rationally.

Phillip watched her and snickered. Yeah, he was *not* the only fretter in the family.

"I think I'll ride over and get Jack. We can make a quick trip over and back, see what's going on."

Elizabeth nodded. "Yes, that'd be good. I'll stay here this time. I need to get some things done. I would like to plan a trip over. I wrote out some more lessons to help Spupaleena in her reading. I also dug up a few good Bible verses to encourage and strengthen her."

"Want me to take them?"

"No, thank you. I need some time with her. I'll go soon. Maybe in a couple weeks. Perhaps you could just let her know I would be coming soon?"

Phillip nodded. "I can do that." He grabbed his Stetson off the wall hook, pulled on his wool coat, hugged his wife, and shuffled out the door.

Elizabeth hummed as she swept up the mud and straw—a never ending chore during the wet spring season. Dry weather could not come fast enough. She peeked at her sleeping children and hurried her pace so she could take in some quiet time reading scripture before they woke up.

It didn't take long for Phillip to reach Jack's sturdy built log cabin. Phillip tied his horse at the hitching post and called for his friend.

"Over here. Putt'n a little salve on a cut." Jack stood, stretching the kinks out of his back.

Phillip rode up and climbed off his horse. "What happened?" He hobbled over to the tied up mare. "How are ya, old girl?" he said, stroking her mane.

"Nothing bad, just got a few wire cuts." Jack gestured to Phillip's leg. "How's it feel'n?"

"Better now that the weather has turned warmer." Phillip grinned wide. "Glad the thugs didn't hack at both my legs when they jumped me. Hav'n one chopped off was about enough."

"That's the truth. What's up, Spup make it over yet?"

"No. That's why I'm here. I think we should ride out in the morning and go check on her and Skumhist. I'm worried he may not be doing the best."

"Yeah, I've been thinking about him too." Jack plucked his cowboy hat off his head and wiped his forehead with the back of his tattered jacket. He adjusted his bandana. "Sounds good to me. I'll be ready first thing."

Phillip nodded. "Good." For some reason a bad feeling kept jabbing at his heart. He needed to see what it was all about, good or bad. Maybe it was nothing, but he had to know.

Chapter 6

Spupaleena felt she had her wits about her. She had Dusty, **Spaoos Newt** ("Heart Breaker") and **Noonwheena** ("Believer") saddled up, ready to practice some exchanges. They would have to take it slow and easy for now. Five weeks was a long time to be off. She felt the need to get back on and push her fright away. Dusty, she knew, had power and confidence, yet was still young enough to work on more control coming in for the catcher. Too many times he wanted to keep going, thinking the whole race was his to run. He knew how to stop, just chose to ignore her and win the race by himself.

Walking over to Noonwheena, an eight-year-old stallion, Spupaleena glided her hand over the sorrel-and-white's back. "You are settled in your ways." She smiled, thankful that he was older and more laid-back. His 15'3 hand frame and strait, sturdy legs carried him fast for the short runs. She learned from him that size had nothing to do with speed. "You certainly can run," she said, her voice filled with adoration. Spupaleena cupped her hands around his bright blue eyes and ran her gentle fingers down his face. The boy could flat out fly. She loved his quickness, his courage, and determination.

She turned and made her way to Spaoos Newt. Yes, he was a heartbreaker. He nickered, knowing there would be a treat. At age eleven, the stallion was at his peak. He was stout and strong, short and full of grit. One word described him—tenacious. Spupaleena looked at him with such love and pride. She scratched his white, bald face. His bay Overo coloring repeatedly captured the eye of his audience. His big, sky-blue eyes were rimmed with pink, healthy flesh.

She was fortunate to have bartered for them both with the whites up north at the Kettle Falls last year during the spring salmon harvest. Women from her village were busy laying out strips of salmon to dry on willow racks in the sun while she traded horses. She, Skumhist, and Pekam had dip netted, speared, and dried enough salmon to bring a fair trade. Her heart warmed as she thought back to her father's satisfied expression as she led the stallions away from their previous owners. She felt he was proud of her decision. There were other horses to pick from, but these two were special. They were well trained, strong, and confident yet calm.

While asking different tasks of the horses, they gladly gave to her. They were soft with quiet eyes and were sure-footed. She had Pekam ride them so she could watch their movements. The pair floated as her brother asked each horse to collect and give to the bit. She had been impressed with their stops, although that was still a work in progress. While they now dribbled down to a nice steady decline, she would be asking for an immediate halt, an easy fix.

She was more impressed with how her scrawny brother handled the stallions. Her eyes had shown bright as he worked the horses. She caught herself smiling more than once as he sat tall and self-assured.

"Hey, Spup, how are things?" Phillip said as the two men rode up to her.

The voice jerked her out of dreamy memories. She looked up, startled, and then smiled gingerly as she saw two of her favorite people. "Oh, Wi, brothers!" Her smile broadened as Jack and Phillip slid off their sweat-covered horses.

The trio embraced.

"You didn't come so we came to you. Is everything all right?" Phillip spoke like an overprotective father.

Spupaleena looked down. She shook her head. "Loot. We had a bad wreck and Pekam wacked his head—again." She moved the dirt with her moccasin-covered foot.

Phillip and Jack exchanged worried glances.

Spupaleena peered at them both, tears pooling in her eyes. She choked them down, willing herself to be strong. She hated to cry, especially in front of the two characters staring at her, mouths gaping open.

"He'll be okay." Her brows lifted and she gave them a small smile.

"No wonder." Phillip said.

"What?" Spupaleena crossed her arms, shifting her weight.

"You've been so heavy on my heart. I felt the Holy Spirit telling me that something was wrong… really wrong."

Jack eyed his partner. He swallowed hard.

Spupaleena was like a daughter to Jack as well and he had freely bred his Paint stallion, Sampson, to her mare so she could start a herd of her own. Jack shifted his gaze to the fresh scar on her forehead. "And you?" he stammered.

"I'm fine." She shrugged her shoulders. "A bump on my head is all. A few scratches. Nothing severe."

Phillip tapped the ground with his walking stick. "And your father?"

Spupaleena squirmed.

Jack cocked his head.

Phillip tapped harder.

"He's upset."

Phillip nodded. "Yeah, I can see why. Maybe you two should not race, just—"

"What? Don't what? Don't say it!" She glared at him, fist clenched ready to swing the first punch.

Jack cleared his throat. "I think what he means… well…to just breed and sell. Stay safe." He stretched out his hands like he was offering her a better deal.

Spupaleena turned to Jack. She felt like grabbing Phillip's walking stick and beating them both over the head. The piercing look on her face made the men want to jump back.

They saw her eyeing the walking stick. Phillip put it in his other hand, the one most out of her reach. She looked at them both. Fuming, she turned on her heels and briskly walked off. They could hear the fringe on her dress swoosh with each stride, fast and furious.

Looking at each other, they shrugged. They quickly high-lined their horses to an existing rope tied between two trees and hurried after the strong-willed girl.

"Wait! Let's talk about this." Jack said in between breaths.

Phillip hobbled as quickly as he could. His leg ached as his frustration picked up the pace. A spasm jolted up his stump and he tumbled to the ground.

Jack stopped but Phillip waved him on.

"Go! I'm okay." Phillip tried to give him a reassuring look. He would catch up.

Hun han neekun had been on a walk and watched the scene unfold from behind some nearby bushes. She had been snickering until she saw Phillip fall. "I'll help him," she hollered as she came out, rushing to his side.

Jack nodded and went after his bull-headed friend.

"Mama," Hannah said; her tone was brash. Her three and one-half foot self stood tall beside her frayed mother. They were outside enjoying the afternoon. There was a break in the stretch of rainy days and a slim ray of sun poked through gray clouds.

Elizabeth handed Delbert a toy cow his father carved for him over the long winter months, sending him off to play. Lillian screeched in the background.

Elizabeth turned to see the toddler lying on her backside, with a shovel on top of her.

"Oh, dear." Elizabeth hurried to her daughter. She stood the crying girl up and wiped the mud off her bundled body.

"Mama, did you hear me?" Hannah placed her mitten covered hands on her slight hips.

"Yes, I did."

"Well, are ya gonna answer me?"

Elizabeth groaned. "In a minute."

Hannah stuck out her bottom lip.

Delbert squealed in delight as he ran across the freshly turned earth that would be the planted garden in a few short months.

Elizabeth stood. She smiled inside at her daughter's persistence. She knew that girl would make it in life off sheer determination. Looking up at the gloomy cloud cover and the single beam of sun struggling to warm the cold, damp earth, she wished for the upcoming summer days with cloudless skies to quickly arrive.

They were all tired of being cooped up in the small cabin in such dreary weather. Only so many books could be read. The children grew tired of playing with the same toys. Fresh air was welcomed. Phillip and Jack would have to add on a room for sure this summer. They needed more space with the additional child. Elizabeth studied the old wooden boards of their cabin. A fresh coat of paint would be nice. They would certainly have their work cut out for them.

Hannah's patience grew thin. "I'm trying to wait, but my insides are tell'n me to speak up."

Elizabeth turned her attention to her precious, brown-haired girl. She tried not to grin. It was important for her to take family matters seriously, but she struggled to keep a sober face gazing down at those big, green eyes under the long, thick lashes. She broke down and smiled anyway.

"I'm ready to discuss your pressing issue now, my dear."

A cheerful expression blossomed on Hannah's face.

Lillian wobbled up and hugged her big sister, giggling with joy. Hannah patted her baby sister affectionately before speaking up. "I wanna race like Auntie Spuppy." The seriousness of her face reflected an age way beyond her tender years.

Elizabeth gasped, covering it up with a cough. She sat for a moment in silence, collecting her thoughts.

"You mean with one horse or three?"

Hannah pondered the question. "With one." She rubbed her face with her scratchy mittens. "Papa can get me one."

"Get you one what? A horse the size of Spupaleena's or one that would suit you better?" Elizabeth thought she would play along for the time being, allowing her unrelenting daughter to really think the issue through.

"Well, it would have to be a pony, one that fits me." She scrunched her nose. "I think my legs would be too short for a big horse."

"You think so?"

"Yeah. A black-and-white pony would match my aunties."

"I see." Elizabeth stifled her desire to burst out laughing. She really didn't want to hurt her daughter's feelings. Even though at times the little girl was challenging, Elizabeth wanted to encourage her passions and her drive to accomplish her dreams, even at her young age. It could only benefit her as a grown woman.

"I saw kids my size racing in her village. I know I can do that. I would be good. I have good blants."

"Blants?"

"Yes, Mama. Blants. You know, so I can stay on my pony gooder."

"Gooder, huh?" Elizabeth tossed her a you-should-know-the-right-word look down at the sheepish-looking girl. "Better is the correct word, and I think you're talking about having good *balance*."

Hannah nodded her head; her round eyes beaming up at her mother.

Elizabeth sat a moment, watching Delbert making mooing noises and twisting his wooden cow around in the muddy soil.

"Well, we'll have to talk to your papa when he returns." *Lord help us,* she thought.

Hannah nodded, and ran off to play with her brother.

Elizabeth sighed deeply, peering down at her round-faced baby girl. "I hope you don't want to race like your sister."

Lillian's cobalt eyes gleamed up at her mother. She grinned as slobber slid down her chin.

"Like I said, Lord help us." Elizabeth glanced up, smiling at the peacefulness of the tree-filled mountains surrounding her.

Pekam was tired of lying in bed. He could hear everyone preparing to ride, but him. He awoke that morning ready to fight for his right to train and when his father entered the dwelling, he jumped at the chance to do battle.

"I'm healed." Pekam stood, glaring into his father's eyes.

"Loot, you are *not* ready to ride." Skumhist's stern look did not sway his son into listening to reason.

"I feel fine. I promised not to do anything stupid and I won't. Everyone else has begun to train; I need to be out there with them. It is my team, remember?"

Spupaleena stumbled as she flew into her father's dome house. She had been eavesdropping outside and burst in, coming to her father's aide. She hated to come against her brother, but it had to be done. This was a serious matter and he was just not getting that through his thick skull—or somewhat mushy head by now. Perhaps that's why he refused to listen to reason.

Father and son turned to face the fuming woman.

She caught her balance and stood tall, squaring her shoulders. "What?" She saw them staring at her. She slammed her fists on her sides.

"We are talking here," Pekam shouted.

Spupaleena glared at her brother, then her father. "Sorry. I didn't know," she stated angrily. "Actually Kewa, I did know. I was listening outside, and—"

"Yeah, well everything isn't about you, Spupaleena." The purple vein lining Pekam's neck looked as if it would explode.

"What? What did I do?"

Skumhist held up his hand. He turned to his daughter. "Nothing." He folded his hands in front of him and turned his attention to his son. "Stop squasee. This squabbling accomplishes nothing."

"I think I'm ready to ride. Maybe not race. You and mistum say I'm not, but I know I am." Pekam crossed his scrawny arms over his chest and arched both of his brows in a defiant manner.

"You aren't ready yet," Spupaleena said matter-of-factly.

"I'll ride again and soon." Pekam stormed out of the tule-mat door, colliding into Jack. They both stumbled. Jack reached to help steady Pekam, but the boy shoved Jack away.

Jack watched the angry twelve-year-old jog off toward the horses. Hearing strained voices in Skumhist's home had made him hesitate to go inside. He could hear the concern in their voices, but failed to hear any words. He leaned closer as a spark of guilt blasted him, knowing it really was not his business.

"What are *you* doing?" A smile creased Phillip's face.

Jack jumped back, fumbling for words. He pointed to the flap. "Oh, nothing. Well, I…I…Pekam ran out this flap like an angry swarm of hornets or something. About ran me over. I was about to go in, but it sounds like you and I need to wait out here until they come out." Jack gestured toward the tule-mat flap with his head.

"I wonder if they're double teaming him. I have a feeling the young lad is chomping at the bit to get back in the saddle," Phillip commented.

Spupaleena stepped out of the pit-house, ramming into the men. "Ouch!"

Startled, the trio backed up and gave each other some space, all looking dazed.

"I'm coming out," Skumhist warned.

Spupaleena shifted to the side, allowing room for her father to enter the brisk morning air.

"How long have you been standing here?" Spupaleena inquired.

"Not long," Phillip answered.

Jack acted like a whipped pup. "I…Pekam ran into me, but I hadn't heard what you said in there. I promise…" He sighed, tipping his Stetson back on his head.

Skumhist smiled and glanced at his daughter, who was also grinning.

Phillip gave Jack a frown, shaking his head. The man was acting like a school boy, not the confident cowboy he knew.

"What's wrong with you?" Phillip asked Jack.

"Nothing." He sneered back.

Skumhist cleared his throat. "Is there something you need to say?"

"No, nothing. Thank you." He nodded at Skumhist.

"I don't have time for this. I need to train." Spupaleena turned to leave but Jack grabbed her arm.

"I do have something to say." Jack stammered, releasing his grip.

Spupaleena relaxed and stood freely.

"I feel somewhat responsible. I've encouraged you to race, and all that seems to happen is you and Pekam end up hurt."

Spupaleena glared at him. "We are *not* hurt." She grabbed her braids and leaned closer to Jack with her dainty face, peering up at him as she stood tip-toed. "Wrecks come with racing and gentling colts. You of all people should know that, but God keeps us safe and alive."

"Safe?" Phillip and Skumhist said in unison.

Spupaleena's face heated as she turned to them. "Yes, safe. We have had bumps and bruises, but we are alive…aren't we? I refuse to cower to fear. It's not from God."

The three men stared at her dumbfounded. The stubborn woman pushed past them and strode to her saddled mounts.

"Lord, make them see this is your will for me. You have protected us…can't they see that?" Spupaleena lifted her chin, mentally preparing herself for the day's workout. Or at least attempting to as she repeatedly pushed away menacing thoughts of her opposing family and friends.

Chapter 7

Elizabeth held Sammy, Phillip's middle-aged Paint horse, while he slid off. He was tired and frustrated and sharp pains electrified his stump of a leg. Four days was enough of Spupaleena's willful demeanor. "How did things go?" she asked.

"Not so great. I think your two weeks need to be pushed ahead. There was another pileup before the first exchange even happened. Pekam hit his head, lost consciousness, and they're both bent on racing soon." He pushed his Stetson back and rubbed his forehead. "Skumhist was right; they should have called the race. The ground was slick as syrup."

Elizabeth ran her fingers along the line separating Sammy's white hair from the black as she listened to her husband relay the details of the horse wreck. She studied the curved pattern on the Paint's neck. "Did anyone suggest they stop racing?"

"Ya, we all did." Phillip winced as he withdrew his Winchester rifle out of the scabbard that was buckled to the saddle. He should have made a point to lean on his good leg.

Elizabeth spoke softly. "Do you think that was the right thing to tell her?"

Phillip shifted his gaze to his wife. He shrugged. "Why not?"

"How did she take it?"

Phillip thought for a moment. "Like a badger gettin' his next meal stolen right out from under him."

"Papa, you're home!" Hannah ran as fast as her little legs would carry her.

Phillip leaned down, arms outstretched. No amount of pain in his leg could stop him from his children's hugs. Hannah hopped up as he scooped her high in the air. She giggled, reaching for his neck to squeeze tightly. His tired muscles screamed at the extra weight.

Elizabeth chuckled, knowing the truth behind the overly, animated greeting.

"Papa, I have something to tell you!" She let out a high-pitched shriek resounding in her father's ear.

"You do?" Phillip chuckled.

"Yes, Papa." The serious expression on Hannah's face spoke loudly.

"Let's get you inside, let your Mama brew me up some of her pain reducing tea, and then you can tell me all about it, okay?"

Hannah wiggled out of his grasp and bolted for the door.

Elizabeth arched a brow and motioned for the door. She snickered to herself. *This should be good.*

By the look on his wife's face, he realized she knew what was about to unfold. He grinned at her, wondering what he was about to commit too. Suddenly he wasn't feeling all that cheerful. He had an inkling his daughter was about to ask him for something he might not approve of. He silently said a quick prayer as he led his horse into the corral, putting the tack away. He stepped out and shut the gate, eyeing his wife and the smirk on her face. They moseyed to the cabin, carrying the bulky packs. All too often, he didn't have the heart to say "no" to his bright-eyed ball of fire. This time he might have to.

It was not long before the other two Gardner children woke up from their naps. Elizabeth corralled the youngest in the kitchen area with baking powder biscuits and milk. Phillip and Hannah sat on a blanket by the glowing fire eating their snacks.

"Papa, I wanna race a pony just like Auntie Spuppy."

Phillip nearly choked on a mouthful of biscuit.

Hannah's eyes grew big and round as she watched her father try and swallow the food lodged in his throat, reaching for a cup of water. All he could find was his wife's tea so he grabbed that, sipping the tepid liquid and blinked away his fear.

"Are you all right, Papa?"

Phillip nodded. "Yes, sweetie, I am." He swallowed hard, making the silence last a bit longer and then took a gulp of water Elizabeth handed him. Looking down at his daughter he asked, "Why, honey, do you want to race?"

"Because my auntie does. I love to watch her win and I wanna win, too." Hannah looked up at her daddy so sweetly, he was tempted to melt inside, gather her in his arms and say....*anything for you darling*. But he knew that would be wrong, not just wrong, but potentially dangerous.

The silence made the girl lower her lashes to the gray wool blanket beneath her and Delbert. Phillip's heart was sinking fast. His daughter was too precious for such a risk.

He took his daughter's tiny hand in his. "Honey, look at me."

Hannah's deep green eyes met her fathers.

"Riding to win is not why your Auntie Spuppy rides. She loves the horses. Winning is the result of her hard work. She rides many hours a day. Her job is anything but easy…okay?"

"I know. I could work hard and ride hard. I'm strong, Papa." Hannah put on the most serious, confident face she could muster up.

"Yes, you are strong. I know you would work hard… but…you see, it can be dangerous." Phillip glanced at Elizabeth, searching for any kind of assistance.

She caught him out of the corner of her eye, but pretended not to notice. She grabbed a nearby book and opened it not really even seeing what was in her hands. Delbert and Lillian took notice and went to be with their mother because she happened to pick up one of their favorite stories. She smiled, but not too big.

Phillip turned his attention back to the little princess sitting in front of him, or should he mean warrior ready to do battle.

"Papa, I know I could get hurt, but won't God protect me? He does Auntie Spuppy. I hear you and Mama say so." She spoke so softly and convincingly. Phillip swallowed hard, struggling to keep a straight face. His daughter's big persuading eyes and soft curls lining her porcelain face captured his heart, causing his attention to swirl. Knowing this was a serious matter, he forced himself to keep a sober face.

"Yes, you're right. God does protect us. He also allows things to happen in our life forcing us to listen to him. He get's our wayward attention back onto him. God will protect us, but not always. The more unsafe activities we do, the higher the chance we can get hurt. That's just part of life." Phillip gathered his little one and pulled her into his protective lap. "I think I have to tell you no, honey. Maybe when you're bigger." *A lot bigger.*

Tears instantly streamed down her cream-colored face. "But I am bigger." She fought hard through cascading tears. "I'm big enough, Papa, I am."

Phillip felt as if his heart was ripping straight out of his chest. "I'm sorry, Hannah. I have to say no." He blinked threatening tears away.

She pushed her way out of his lap and ran to her bed.

Phillip remained on the blanket. He could never forgive himself if she ever got hurt. The way he found Spupaleena lying lifeless that winter day, six years ago, haunted him. He could never find Hannah in a bad way. He wiped his face with his flannel shirt sleeve and stared into the crackling fire.

Spupaleena left the men in a huff. She took hold of Dusty's lead rope and then reached down and grasped the tightly braided lead ropes of the other two stallions off the top pole of her sturdy corral. Drizzling afternoon rain soaked her doeskin dress, but she felt nothing. Nothing but rage peppered with confusion. Perhaps the cool rain would put out the fire in her soul. *How could they suggest I quit? I have worked too hard; rode too many hours. I have fought too hard. No. I will not quit!*

She urged Dusty forward hoping Noonwheena and Spaoos Newt would follow, but instead, they bit and kicked at each other. Dusty pinned his ears and kicked at the pair with his back legs. Spupaleena jerked the lead ropes in order to catch their attention, but the fighting only exploded. Before she could count to **naux** ("One"), total mayhem detonated, having the force of an erupting volcano.

Horses squealed—rearing, striking, biting, ripping the lead ropes out of her hands. She was able to whirl Dusty around. *There's no way I can get control back. What was I thinking? Ponying stallions together doesn't work—ever. How brainless could I be?*

Skumhist, Pekam, the other racers, cousins…they all came running, shooing nearby children away from the dangerous, kicking hooves. Some stood with their hands up in the air, not quite knowing what to do. Then, from nowhere came two distinct voices.

"Spaoos Newt," hollered K̲ook Yuma In-tee-tee-huh.

"Whoa now, Noonwheena." Chy chy pum Sn'e stepped at an angle that the stallion could catch a glimpse of him out of the corner of the horse's right eye.

Both catchers lifted their hands as if they were ready to catch the horses at the exchange sites. Again they called the names of the stallions Spupaleena had galloped to them each and every day. The horses's ears turned to their respective handlers. They quit rearing. Snorting and huffing sounds still came from the horses, but they stood still, gazing at the catchers.

A hush settled over the on lookers. No sound could be heard. Not a cry of a baby. Not a bark of a dog. Nothing. No one.

The catchers turned and caught the outside eye of their horses. Noonwheena snorted and shook his head. Spaoos Newt pawed the ground with his front hoof and he tossed his head. Only the settling rustle of the horses's hooves on soggy ground could be heard.

Spupaleena kept Dusty quiet so the boys could keep the horses' attention. He seemed to watch intently, ears pricked forward.

Skumhist stood amazed at what his eyes were seeing.

Pekam smiled, hands on his hips, feet spread shoulder width, chin slightly elevated.

The stallions settled down, their ears pinned on the catchers, who reeled them in with their soft, horse-like manner. The studs took step after step toward the distinct voice they knew so keenly from the exchanges. The voice they counted on to bring them in. They knew their catcher's voice, smell, face. The quiet strength pulled them in like a magnet. Finally, each man reached out, clutching the rope, gently asking the horse to come into them.

Reaching out, the men rubbed the head and neck of their horse and spoke to them softly, caringly. The horses lowered their heads, licking their lips in submission. They stood quiet.

A huge smile broke out on Spupaleena's face. She was fortunate to have such horsemen on her team. She admired their skill and patience. Suddenly familiar thoughts assaulted her mind and the smile was replaced with a frown. Chastising impressions flooded her. *How could you have done that? What were you thinking? Someone could have been hurt.*

These malicious notions swiftly swept her merriment away. Her head bowed, not in prayer, but shame. She could feel the criticizing eyes burrowing a hole straight through her gut. She was normally so careful. Immersed in her disgrace, she felt a hand on her knee. Looking down, she saw her brother's caring eyes peering up at her. He stood, grinning. No words were necessary. They knew what the other thought and felt. The siblings were so much alike, in so many ways.

Spupaleena turned her attention to her father, who stood glaring at them. She gasped, making Pekam turn his head. A look of surprise crossed his face.

Dusty fidgeted, feeling his owner's tension. Spupaleena whirled him around, nearly knocking Pekam to the ground. She kicked him into a gallop and sped off. Her body trembled. She clutched the reins as a feeling of worthlessness cascaded over her. Was it asking too much for a little support? Some forgiveness?

Finally, several miles later, Dusty trickled down to a walk and Spupaleena reined him to a stop. She slipped off his back, dropping to her knees. Releasing the rein, she let her head fall into her hands.

Embarrassment, rage, regret—it all swirled around her like a horrifying nightmare. The pit in Spupaleena's stomach grew and she felt nauseated. As her willful spirit began to weaken, the Holy Spirit began to uplift her heart. Now that she was alone, her spirit was open to God's spirit—his voice. She prayed for wisdom and peace, what she always seemed to pray for. Soon her shoulders relaxed. Warmth tingled up her body, surrounding her like a warm blanket. Her thoughts changed from menacing to encouraging. *It's all right, daughter. No one was hurt. You will learn from this and become stronger.*

Tears flowed from relief, peace, and comfort that came from a place no human had the power to emulate. Her arms and legs now grew limp. She looked up, stood, and crawled back on her stallion. "Lim lumt, God. You're right; there is no room for pity. My strength comes from you alone." She waved her legs asking for Dusty to walk. "Kewa, Elizabeth has shared this with me, from your word: here on earth we will have many trials and sorrows. But take heart, because you Lord have overcome the world." Spupaleena smiled, wiped her eyes with her sleeve and headed home.

Dark was fast approaching and the cool air turned to a frigid bite. Her face stung, as did her fingers. Dusty grunted and huffed as he picked his way through the dense forest floor. Spupaleena reached down and stroked his neck. She could barely see the outline of his black, fuzzy ears. Her teeth started to chatter. She shook, attempting to rid the chill chiseling her bones. She leaned down, half laying across Dusty's neck, sharing his heat. The horn on the saddle pressed against her stomach, but she was able to hunker down enough to stay warmer, plunging her fingers into his fluffy hair.

Pitter-pattering sounds of the night resonated through the tree lined path. Squirrels scurried to their beds. Birds tucked into their nests. Fox and other predators found warmth in their dens. Spupaleena was thankful that a horse's night vision was exceptional.

"Soon, we'll be home and warm," Spupaleena reassured Dusty. They quickly came to the valley that was a mere couple miles from the village. Spupaleena knew the trail was free of holes and harmful debris so she urged her horse into a trot. He gladly accepted and picked up the pace.

As she approached the tule-pit homes, Spupaleena noticed the silence that hung in the air and instantly felt alarm. Frantically eyeing the empty homes throughout the village for any morsel of existence, she and Dusty quietly zigzagged their way down the scattered lane of dwellings, searching for any sign of life. She heard nothing. She saw nothing. The pair meandered a bit further and stopped.

A faint light caught her attention at the other end of the village. Peering closer, she saw what looked like bodies hovering over something. She could see a soft glow of someone holding a torch and it looked like a trace of movement shuffling around. She sat still for a few minutes, cocking her head, willing sound to enter her ears.

Silence. She bumped her calves on Dusty's sides and he walked toward the light.

Chapter 8

Elizabeth stood hunched over the kitchen table as she organized her belongings. She gathered a chalkboard, chalk, her Bible, other children's books, warm clothing for her and the children, herbs and rubs. This time, she would make sure Spupaleena could at least learn enough letters and sounds to start reading some easy Bible verses and simple children's books. The women had been working on letters and numbers for some time now, but only in spurts, so not much had been accomplished.

Knowing how frustrated her friend was about not being able to sufficiently read, Elizabeth made sure to pack reading materials that would set Spupaleena up for success. She even created a word and picture list to help set the letters deep into her memory. She hummed as she organized and carefully placed the items in her horse pack.

Phillip lugged in minimal camping supplies ready for the pack horse. They wouldn't have to bring too much as Skumhist would supply most of their needs. He laid out his goods on the floor in front of the crackling fire. The house filled with the sweet scent of larch wood burning in the fireplace, one of the most pleasing aromas in the territory. He breathed in the scent and grinned.

Phillip was kneeling on the wooden floor sifting through his packs, Delbert kneeling at his side, a mirror image. He pulled out an old piece of hide from one of the packs and unrolled it. He smiled and looked up at his wife. He stood, walking to her, holding out the piece of hide. His son toddling behind him with a handkerchief in hand that was pulled from a pack, just like his pa.

She glanced over her shoulder and looked at him. "What?"

"My rider's list…" Phillip beamed like a young child with an art project.

"Don't you need to add to it?"

"Yeah, that's why I'm bringing it. Spupaleena can help me finish it."

Elizabeth turned, plunked her hands on her hips and stared at her husband. "I still can't figure out why you and Jack are so fixated on that list when she has such a hard time with letters."

"She'll learn. We can help teach her too, ya know."

Elizabeth tossed her head back and laughed. "Oh, I am truly excited to witness this. Make sure I'm around for it, please."

"I will!" Phillip grunted and went back to his place on the floor. Delbert reached out his chubby little hands, giving his mama the handkerchief, babbled some words and joined his pa.

The Gardners took that day to pack and plan the half-day's ride to the village of Spupaleena's **Sinyekst** ("Speckled Fish") people. They would leave in the morning, after a hearty breakfast and strap Lillian on Phillip's back. Delbert rode in front of his pa and Hannah rode with her mama.

It all worked fine for now, but soon, Hannah would need her own horse, better yet, pony. She was getting too big to ride with Elizabeth for the longer journeys; the saddle was just too cramped. But now with the interest in racing, her parents hesitated. They fought to protect their little girl from harm. They agreed with little ponies that merely trotted, the risk was minimal at best. But they feared once the strong-willed ball of fire got a taste of the thrill that came with pony racing, she would be hooked for life, just like her Auntie Spuppy.

Elizabeth understood the little girl's need for independence, but racing was taking the meaning a bit too far. It was one thing for Spupaleena to race. Her balance and athleticism was spot on. She was practically born in the woods, or the saddle in this case, and she really didn't belong to the Gardners, not by blood anyhow. Yes, love had fused their hearts together, but blood separated their lives. Elizabeth shuddered every time Hannah's little voice crept into her mind, *Can I race, daddy?* It was just too much.

Phillip, on the other hand, almost came unglued. His gut wrenched with the haunting question. He constantly beat it out of his thoughts. He relived finding Spupaleena that blustering winter day over and over again in his mind, as well as the time he and Jack had her out for the first time on Dusty. They were going to surprise her with a fun day filled with, "playing with cows." A cougar had jumped them and the stud colt bolted. They finally found her unconscious, and her horse was nowhere to be found. And now, the first wreck of the season, not to mention the first race of the season.

There were so many accidents. No, they had to protect Hannah from her desires and turn her onto a better path—a safer path. Elizabeth hated to admit it; woman's work was a fulfilling pleasure. Not a duty, but a privilege. Taking care of her family thrilled the woman. She secretly hoped that one day, Spupaleena would settle down with a husband and children. She knew her sister would love a family of her own as much as she loved the Gardners. Perhaps not immediately, but someday she would find the joys that came with a woman's life as wife and mother.

The April night was cold and damp. There were no clouds to hold in the warmth from the longer days. The sky glowed with a silver moonlight and a heaven full of twinkling stars that guided the nighttime critters—all of them.

"Come on, let's go!" Hahoola<u>who</u> motioned his two cohorts over with a jerk of his head.

Toople nodded. "Almost done."

Swas Kee eagerly searched for anyone who might be lurking around a dark corner. He was hunkered down near Toople, twitching like a bird pecking at a worm. What a sight he was. His buckskin looked like it had never been washed, and it smelled just as bad.

Toople looked at him and frowned. "Hold still! You'll wake up the entire village."

Swas Kee nodded. His head jerked a few more times before he was able to still his jolting movements.

The full moon gave off plenty of light. They were almost done. The haunting glow off the fool's charcoal eyes fueled the fire in Swas Kee's stonecold heart. He was more excited about the work done that night than Hahoolawho was. The fool's heart dealt with revenge. Swas Kee's motives purely desired to please his uncanny leader.

Hahoolawho put his hand up, alarmed from a crackling noise. Swas Kee waved at Toople, who was mere inches away, motioning him to hold quiet. The trio froze, straining their ears for the slightest sound. Minutes passed as one boy looked to the other. Toople watched the figure in front of him, laying his hands on it making sure nothing broke the silence.

"Hurry, we must go, *now*," Hahoolawho whispered. He glared at Toople in a way that sent chills down his already frigid self. His face looked disfigured and painfully violent.

Toople smiled. "Coming." He enjoyed making the fool squirm. He could also control the situation and wasn't about to let Hahoolawho have all the glory.

Scooping up their possessions, the three scattered like chickens chased by a fox. The only difference was that no sound was made. They knew the falling snow would cover their tracks. All that was left was the silence and eeriness of demise.

One by one the crowd peered up at Spupaleena and moved to the side. She warily made her way to the center. Chills formed on her arms and ran up her neck to the top of her head. She shook them off. Family and friends stared at her with concern stamped on their faces. Spupaleena walked on as a pit formed in her stomach. Her mouth went dry. She grabbed her braids and held on tight.

Shock crossed her face as the observers parted and what she feared came into view. She dropped to the ground. "Loot!" she cried.

Simill<u>k</u>ameen was already treating the near dead horses with some putrid-smelling herbal concoction.

"Where were you, <u>lth</u>kickha?" Pekam glared at his sister. Detestation radiated from his eyes. "We seem to always be searching for you. You have little consideration for anyone, but yourself. You're never here when we need you, when they need you." Pekam pointed to the horses that lay in the snow, straining with each breath.

Spupaleena gasped at her brother's sharp words; her stomach clenched. Tears pooled at the base of her eyes.

She blinked, letting them slip down her hot cheeks. She turned to her father, for once not caring who saw her cry. "What happened? I only went to clear my head and ask God to forgive my thoughtless actions. Who did this?" A lump in her throat caused the words to come out in a whisper.

Skumhist shook his head. "We don't know." He raised his gaze to her. "Hun han neekun found them. After dinner she went to rub them down with the medicine you've been using. They were missing from their corrals—all of them. She looked around and found nothing. She came and got me and the rest of the teammates. We all searched until we found them… here in the trees…like this." Skumhist gestured with his arm toward the horses.

Simill<u>k</u>ameen went from horse to horse with her herbal medicines. <u>K</u>oo<u>k</u>yuma In-tee-tee-<u>huh</u> and Chy chy pum Sn'e helped hold the horses' limp heads up high enough for the healer to pour the burning liquid down their throats. It took both boys to hold the dead weight up. The poor animals were barely alive, but they were breathing.

Spupaleena sat frozen—numb. She quietly watched Simill<u>k</u>ameen care for her horses. She should be the one trying to save their lives. No! She should have stayed. This would not have happened if she had only stayed. "Oh, Creator God, please forgive me. Punish me, not them. Let them live. It's my fault. Forgive my selfishness. Forgive my…my…" Sobs choked her words to silence.

Spupaleena caught the look of an elder, glaring at her, shaking her head. Her mouth was moving, but no words could be heard, at least not by Spupaleena. Looking about, she saw every eye on her. Frowns were worn on every face. Spupaleena reached out, but stopped herself. Her head spun like a whirlwind. She tried to stand, but an unknown force stopped her. A nauseous feeling swept over her and she fell back into the lap of someone kneeling behind her.

Late that night, Spupaleena woke to familiar voices whispering nearby. *Elizabeth is that you?* She didn't have the strength nor will to speak audibly. Her thoughts graciously reminded her of last night's nightmare. *Was it true? Were the horses poisoned?* At least that's what it appeared to her. Otherwise the healer would not be pouring medicine into them. She wondered if they had gotten into some bad weeds. Or…no. Her mind was irrational. *Could someone have? Loot! Stop. No one would dare harm them.* Not that many. Not her and Pekam's entire team.

Struggling to open her eyelids, she jerked her head. "Why would anyone want to hurt them?"

"Spupaleena? Are you awake?" Elizabeth scurried to her side. She dipped a cloth into a finely crafted wood bowl and patted down her friend's forehead. Cool water dribbled down the side of Spupaleena's face. The coolness was refreshing on her overheated skin.

"Kewa." She opened her eyes slightly, peering up at Elizabeth. "When did you get here?" She questioned.

"Not long ago." Elizabeth continued to soothe her friend with cool water.

A tear slipped down Spupaleena's cheek. "Did you… did…" Guilt made it impossible to continue.

"I did." Elizabeth lifted her eyes to Skumhist who stooped on the other side of Spupaleena. "Your father filled me in." She gazed down at Spupaleena and smiled. "You fainted."

"How long have I been asleep?"

"For many hours." Skumhist tilted his head. "Since last night. And it's almost time for our midday meal," he answered.

Closing her eyes, Spupaleena covered her face with her arms, chastising herself for running off and allowing someone to sneak in and harm their horses, if they really did, and for fainting before the entire village. *How brainless could I be? What kind of example am I setting for other young women, let alone as a believer in God?*

"Kewa, by the look on your face, you regret your actions." Skumhist paused, offering his daughter a chance to respond. She nodded, remaining silent. "Running off has never gotten you very far, even though you continue to do so. But what happened to the horses is not your fault." Skumhist glanced at Elizabeth who was nodding her head in agreement. "It could have happened to anyone at anytime."

"He's right. It could happen to you, Skumhist. It could happen to us or Jack. What we need to do now is figure out who did this and why." Elizabeth picked up a brush and began to run its bristles through Spupaleena's hair.

"Do you think someone poisoned them?" Spupaleena pursed her lips in anger.

"Kewa. There is no bad feed they could've eaten. Plus"—Skumhist held out an open scrap of buckskin—"we found poisonous herbs wrapped in this. It was left behind."

Spupaleena grabbed the herbs out of her father's hands, leather and all, and stood, letting out a gut-wrenching grunt that came from a place so far down in her spirit, she even shocked herself. She balled her hands into a fist and jabbed at the air. "Someone will pay for this!"

Red-faced and big-eyed, she rushed out of the tule-pit house and scurried off. The fringe of her doeskin dress hammered her body, trying to keep pace with her scornful steps. She walked down to the river and sat on a stump-sized piece of driftwood. Her body was heated even though the air surrounding her was cool. She picked up a handful of pebbles and tossed them into the river. She was dizzy and weak, but was too angry to lie down.

The expanding ripples in the smooth flowing river reminded Spupaleena that her anger could end up the same way if she didn't reel it in. The next thing she would see would be the same contempt trickle down to her teammates and Pekam and his team. Her brother was already riding a three-foot wave; he needed no help creating a larger swell. All it took was one stone to create a tsunami and she thought better than to be that stone.

She sat and prayed for trust and control, two attributes she could not gather on her own. Hearing footsteps coming up behind her, Spupaleena smiled knowing they were Elizabeth's.

"Mind if I sit a moment?"

"Loot, of course not." Spupaleena picked up a stick and began drawing crude pictures of horses in the sand. They appeared to be like the Anasazi pictographs of the southwest Natives.

Elizabeth spread out an old tattered quilt and sat down. She stretched her legs out, resting back on her elbows. "I can't believe I'm about to say this." She glanced over at her friend and smiled. "You need to get back on a horse."

Spupaleena chuckled as she continued to doodle in the sand. "You know me too well."

She spoke without changing her gaze from the drawings.

"You won't be happy doing anything else."

Spupaleena grunted in agreement.

"What're you going to do now?" Elizabeth crossed her ankles, leaning back against the driftwood that Spupaleena sat on.

"I've been thinking. I know this sounds like it might be for the wrong reasons…but, I want to bring Quiy Sket back over and train him. Give Dusty a rest." She scrunched her nose and raised her eyelashes to her trusted confidant. "What do you think?"

Elizabeth ran her fingers through the soft, wet sand. "I think you need to make that decision on your own."

Spupaleena nodded.

"Only you know your motives."

Silence filled the air.

Spupaleena gazed at the river's leisurely current. She sighed. "I want a horse that has already run. One I don't need to put extra work into. He knows the ropes. I just…"

Elizabeth turned to face Spupaleena. "Just what?"

"Well, he can run, that's for sure, but he hasn't really had much, if any, practice with the exchanges. The poisoning makes me realize having a back up horse might be a good idea."

"How do you think he'll do?"

Spupaleena tossed the stick aside. "I think he'll do great. Jack keeps him ridden and working cows. He has a good, quiet mind now that he can relax knowing no one is out to mistreat him."

"Mmm." Elizabeth nodded in agreement.

"I can't help thinking…this could have happened to Dusty if I hadn't taken off. He could have been dead."

"Yes, he could have, but he's not. This time running off actually was a good thing." Elizabeth couldn't believe those words slipped out of her mouth.

Spupaleena jumped up and held out her hand to Elizabeth.

"Kewa, first thing in the morning, I'll take Rainbow and go get the stallion." Her eyes sparkled with glee.

Elizabeth placed her hand in her friends and Spupaleena pulled her up. They giggled like school girls as Elizabeth hugged Spupaleena. Elizabeth scooped up the blanket and they headed back.

"So…ready for a few lessons tonight before the big work out?"

"Sure. That sounds fine." Spupaleena stopped and turned to Elizabeth.

"Oh, I forgot." Spupaleena suddenly felt heat rise in her neck. "Well, it's about Hannah."

"Yeah?" A knowing feeling came over Elizabeth and ran straight down her spine.

"She asked me to find her a pony, and that you and Phillip said she could race."

Elizabeth's mouth shot open. "What? She lied."

"That's what I figured."

"Oh, when we get back…I'm gonna…she's gonna…"

Spupaleena grabbed Elizabeth's hand and led her back home. She knew her sister was fuming inside because her hand kept twitching as she was sure the woman was scolding her daughter with tongue lashing thoughts.

Chapter 9

The sun cast a pink glow in the sky as it was also waking up, not yet up over the mountain tops. The morning air felt warm on Spupaleena's cheeks. There was a light breeze and she stole a moment to lift up her face, close her eyes, and let the gentle wind brush against her skin. She was feeling the pressure of having her training schedule well overdue, but allowed herself to take a moment to enjoy God's creation.

Standing still, Spupaleena closed her eyes and said a silent prayer. She stood in the stillness of the early morning only to hear hushed voices in the background as adults began to stir and ready themselves for a day of hard work. Village life was all about survival: hunting, fishing, gathering berries and roots and herbs, tanning hides.

Glancing around, there was no sign of Elizabeth, Phillip, or her father. That was good. They needed their rest. Skumhist had been strained with caring for Pekam—again. Attempting to corral the boy's anger and will for revenge was no easy task. With three rambunctious children, the Gardners were likely exhausted. The extra sleep would certainly strengthen their immune system, allowing them to keep up.

Spupaleena stretched her arms up, then from side to side. She bent over, touching her finger tips to the ground. She strolled over to Rainbow's corral and plunked one foot on the second to lowest pole and leaned over, stretching her hamstring, then switched legs.

She learned quickly that her own limberness was a huge factor for a smooth exchange. After the first few days of training, she felt the stiffness in her body from a lack of adequate stretching. She learned her lesson and never again cheated herself. Once Jack showed her what to do, she kept it up; even during seasons she was scarcely riding.

Standing straight with her eyes closed, head bent and relaxed, she let her arms hang at her sides and drew in a deep breath, allowing her lungs to expand completely, held it in a moment and then blew it out her pursed lips. She felt the tension in her shoulders and neck release and slip away like the morning fog. She moved her neck slowly from side to side, breathing steadily.

Courage, strength, direction—it all filled her up like a good, hearty meal. She lifted her head and opened her dark, fiery eyes. A smile broke out across her face. She reached for Rainbow's halter and opened the corral gate. Her chestnut mare whinnied and walked over to her owner, nosing for a treat. Spupaleena pulled out a handful of wild carrots and held her hand out flat.

Rainbow gently picked the sweet treat out of Spupaleena's hand with her soft mouth. Spupaleena giggled and rubbed the horse down with her hands before tacking her up and heading out. Rainbow stretched her neck and twisted her head in delight. Spupaleena missed this special time with her mare.

It wasn't long before they were at the water crossing at the Columbia River. It was more dangerous than normal this time of year. High snow-packed mountains melted and a deluge of water rushed down the creeks that flowed into the mighty Columbia. The rapidly swelling river seemed to go from knee deep to neck deep in just a few short weeks.

Spupaleena scanned the passage, searching for the best approach. She sat, wondering how the Gardners made it with the children. Did they have problems that were kept from her? Good thing Hannah was riding with her mother and not a pony that would have been swept away with the current. She shuddered at the thought and would have to inquire about it when she returned.

After deciding on the best way to go about crossing the liquid beast, Spupaleena waved her legs, asking Rainbow to move forward. The mare craned her neck back and shook her head. The noise that came from Spupaleena's throat was a blend of surprise and impatience. The mare had crossed this path many times. Her balking had to be nothing short of old age.

Spupaleena rubbed the horse's neck reassuringly and urged her forward once again. The mare pawed and snorted.

"What is it girl?"

Rainbow twirled around, dancing and crow hopping, trying her best to evade the water.

"Whoa," Spupaleena said, attempting to keep her tone in check.

Spupaleena investigated the area for any sign that would frighten the mare. At the same time, she took hold of the reins and tried to steady her mount, talking softly. She was about ready to break out in a quiet lullaby when she heard the sharp growl of an angry bear.

The massive black form came at her, standing on his haunches and shaking his thick neck slowly back and forth. Rainbow reared and came down quivering, stomping her feet. Normally the bear would not have even blinked at the site of a human, however this time of year, when the earth is warming and the cranky creatures are waking up from a winter of slumber, standing between them and their smorgasbord of fresh salmon, well, wasn't the best position to be in.

The only thing Spupaleena could think to do when the vicious monster began to lunge at them, baring his jagged teeth, was to turn and run! But instead of hightailing it deep into the woods, or back to the safety of her warm pit-home, she dashed straight for the bulging river.

The beast charged forward.

Rainbow squealed and side stepped at the river line, terror squeezing in on her. The mare broke out into a sweat that soaked her body. There was no time to lull the horse into the frigid water. Instead, Spupaleena grabbed the end of her rein and popped the quivering animal on the rump making a sharp cracking sound.

Spupaleena cringed and hung on. "Sorry girl—time to save our lives."

Rainbow suddenly plunged into the water. She had swum this river plenty of times. The only difference was that no bear had wanted her for lunch.

Spupaleena leaned forward allowing the mare to have her head. They were drifting quickly, picking up speed with the swift current. Spupaleena felt Rainbow tipping sideways, so she shifted her weight to offset the current and help hold the struggling mare upright. If the horse's legs swung up, they would be swept down the river and would surely drown.

Rainbow strained, swimming like a minx that had fallen off the ledge of a cliff. Her breaths came in short gasps as she stretched her neck and fought for control.

They were almost there. Spupaleena prayed as they swam the last several yards. The only problem was the pair drifted past the point where they normally came out of the water and onto the nice sandy patch of land. Spupaleena searched the area for a suitable place to get out. She saw only steep, brushy banks. Soon Rainbow would be able to touch, but it would be worthless if there was nowhere to go.

Panic jabbed at her, threatening to take over. "Loot! Help us Lord…" Spupaleena was losing her grip, but with a slight shift in balance was able to regain it. Her knees gripped the mare's sides, and she clung tight to the exhausted animal.

There was one more bend and maybe—just maybe—there would be a flat piece of ground to climb up on.

The river floor came into contact with distressed hooves. The mare lunged forward, ramming into the bank that blocked her way out of the pulsating monster. The mare screamed as she frantically tried to climb her way from the claws she was sure were trying to suck her back down into the dark, wet den. Spupaleena took hold of the reins and whirled her around, kicking her back into the water. Rainbow plunged back in, nearly falling to her knees.

There was a mere inch of dry land between the bank and the river, and the horse was able to take two ankle-deep steps before pitching off the drop-off and back to swimming breathlessly.

"Sorry girl, we'll make it. You'll see." Spupaleena had to swallow all her fears so Rainbow could seize an ounce of bravery.

Glancing back, Spupaleena saw the massive black bear sitting leisurely on the bank. He was watching them and waved a paw in the air as if to say, "Thanks and see ya later." Spupaleena grunted and turned her attention back to finding that spot they could finally get out of the freezing water and onto dry land. They were both exhausted and cold and frustration was eating at both horse and human.

Looking ahead, Spupaleena could see they were almost to the bend. "Come on, Rainbow, you can do it," she said encouragingly. Rubbing the old girl's mane and neck, she felt the mare regain some gumption and move steadily along. That mare would do anything for her beloved owner. The bond they had formed on the journey home five years prior from the Gardners was pivotal. Spupaleena promised herself that she would never take this beauty, with a heart of courage, for granted; her passion was too great.

"Here it is!" Spupaleena broke out into a wide grin, and her tense muscles began to relax. The current propelled them around the corner and it wasn't long before Rainbow felt solid ground and sighed deeply. They had made it.

Spupaleena patted Rainbow's neck and cheered with joy. They crawled up onto the grassy bank. Spupaleena slid off her mare and kissed the ground. She rolled over onto her back and closed her eyes. "Thank you, Father, for protecting us…" She felt a huge wave of gratitude come over her. She lay on the ground careful not to fall asleep and freeze in her sopping wet clothing. She turned her head and watched her faithful mare.

Rainbow's breathing quieted after some time and she wandered over to a close patch of fresh green grass that was just beginning to poke out of the soggy ground, clipping the short blades off with her sharp front teeth. Lifting her head, she snorted, and then went back to ravaging her meal.

Spupaleena started a crackling fire to warm up and dry off her drenched clothing. Her teeth finally stopped rattling and her body ceased to shake. She pinched some mint tea into a tin cup of steaming water, slowly sipping the hot drink. That was one episode she hadn't counted on nor ever wished to repeat.

Jack lifted his head at the sound of fluid hoof beats trotting up the lane to his simple, tidy home. Everything had its place and he made sure things were in that place. Being a bachelor allowed that kind of time. He sat in his three box stall barn on a sturdy pine stool washing and oiling his saddles and bridles, preparing them for the spring rains. The door laid open, letting a fresh breeze waft in, airing out the stuffy, hay dusted area.

Jack smiled, knowing the familiar clopping sound of the laid-back mare he had given the Native girl. He hadn't expected her visit, but was delighted nonetheless. She was like the daughter he never had. He and his deceased wife had two sons, who now were also with the Lord. Jack preferred to keep his deceased family to himself. Talking about it only made him wish he were in heaven with them.

God had given him precious time with them on earth and he knew the separation was only temporary. They would all be together someday, together forever. Only the Creator knew that day, so he made the choice to live the rest of his time celebrating life. There was just too much to be thankful for. He was a mighty God who only wanted blessings for his children. Nothing was too big for Him, and Jack had little patience for those who sat around feeling sorry for themselves.

"Hey, there." Spupaleena rode up still damp from their excursion.

Jack stood with a smirk. He looked her and Rainbow over not knowing whether to laugh or ask questions first. Or just wait and let the girl tell her story. Her doeskin dress was covered in dried mud and her braids were beginning to unravel.

Noticing the expression on Jack's face, she lowered her lashes in embarrassment.

Jack arched his thick eyebrows and tipped his Stetson back on his head.

"We took an unexpected swim." Spupaleena twisted her hands as she sat in the saddle, suddenly aware of how scruffy she appeared. She grabbed her braids and held on tight.

Jack stood watching her squirm for a minute then reached out a hand to help her down. He grinned. "Must have been a good one."

Spupaleena giggled and handed him her pack. "I'll fill you in over a hot cup of tea."

"You got it."

The heat of the tin cup warmed Spupaleena's tingling fingers. Her nose ran from the cold, but her bones were finally thawing out as she sat by the roaring fire, bundled in a wool blanket wrapped around her hunched over shoulders.

She retold the story as they sat by the fire. Jack laughed heartily. *Yep, if I had a daughter, she would be just like Spup*, he told himself. He sat listening to the story, admiring her courage and determination.

Spupaleena chuckled as she thought about the dumb old bear waving its good-riddance.

She was so tired, but the thrill of coming to bring Quiy S<u>k</u>et home kept her pulse humming. She dabbed her dripping nose with a laced handkerchief Jack handed her. She figured it must have been one of his wife's. Spupaleena wished she had met her. She must have been a remarkable woman. Since Jack rarely spoke of his family, she would never know and would never ask.

"I was surprised to see you." Jack sat across from the girl, tapping his long fingers on the table.

Spupaleena stared at his rapping hand with an annoyed look on her face and Jack stopped. It was a habit that soothed his mind. He glanced down at his mud-caked boots and chastised himself for not leaving them at the door.

Spupaleena shifted in her chair. "I came to get my stallion." Her tone suddenly turned impatient.

Jack snapped his head up. "What? Why? What's going on?"

"You'll never believe it."

"Try me..."

Spupaleena sighed in aggravation. She relayed all that had happened down to who they all pinned the blame on, at least she did.

Jack nodded in disbelief. "He does seem to be the obvious target."

"Who else could it be? Who else has reason to stop us from racing?"

"Someone who's jealous of you—a woman rider. Actually that could be man or woman. Just because he's the likely candidate, doesn't mean he's the one who poisoned your horses, if they were poisoned at all."

Spupaleena pursed her lips and she looked away. "They were poisoned." She locked her gaze on Jack, narrowing her eyes with sheer determination and detestation, and spoke, "I *know* it was the fool!"

Jack jerked back. He'd never seen this kind of loathing in his friend. Her face twisted with resentment. It was a far cry from the kind, loving look of friendship and respect when she first rode up. Jack prayed for wisdom. He was so taken back, his mouth opened, but nothing came out so he clamped it shut.

They sat in silence for a few minutes—Jack stared blankly at her, and Spupaleena's dark and fiery eyes looked past him to some unknown place. The only sound in the room was the popping fire.

Finally Jack stood, refreshed their cups of tea and sat back down with a hard thunk. He set Spupaleena's tea in front of her. She watched the steam swirling out of her cup like the harsh thoughts rambling in her mind.

Jack plunked his tin cup on the wood table and looked at Spupaleena sternly. "What're you thinking of doing? I hope nothing, because this…"

Spupaleena wasn't listening. She had a plan, but questioned if it was the time to share it just now. Jack's fingers tapping on the table pulled her back to the conversation. She glanced up and gave him a small smile. "Our horses are still recovering, so I'm going to bring in the stallion. I was with Dusty in the mountains at the time, so he's okay…" her voice trailed off as she seemed to glare at her cup.

Jack nodded. "Don't you need two other horses? Or I guess just one if Dusty's okay."

Spupaleena eyes darted back to Jack. "Kewa. Two. I'm letting Dusty rest. I figure having a back up horse might not be a bad idea."

Jack nodded. "Well?" Jack knew something was stirring in that stubborn mind of hers. Good or bad, it was bubbling and ready to spill out.

Spupaleena nodded. "We have two borrowed horses we're going to use. I just need Quiy Sket either for the start or last leg, haven't decided which yet. With his speed and quickness off the start line, we'll hold our own." Her eyes brightened.

"Hold your own?" Jack smirked. "What are you planning? Nothing good comes out of—"

"Nothing, Jack! I'm planning nothing, but continuing to train and I need a strong, sturdy horse. He's mine; I won him and want to use him. What harm is there in using my own horse? I race, Jack. That's what I do. I need to get him and get back. We have a lot of catching up to do." Spupaleena trembled with anger, pausing to catch her breath. "Can I leave Rainbow here for awhile?" She fingered the ends of the blanket that were wrapped around her sagging shoulders.

Jack felt like he had just been slapped in the face. He sat stunned. *No plan my...*

"Can I?" Her voice softened.

Silence hung in the room.

She pushed her chair back and stood, biting her lip.

Jack nodded, his eyes filled with concern. "Ya… Okay…I guess."

"Lim lumt. It won't be long. A few weeks maybe."

"Fine. Spupaleena—"

She dropped her blanket on the chair, turned on her heels, and rushed to the door, snatching her pack on the way out. She couldn't get out of the cabin quick enough. She hated to lie to Jack, but was it really lying, or just withholding information? There was no harm in keeping her plan tucked away in her head. Did she really have a plan? Or was she just letting the wind blow in whatever bitter direction it chooses to carry her?

Elizabeth had warned her about letting her emotions control her rationale, but she was right. The fool was responsible for the poisoning. No one else hated her like he did and no one else had reason to. She would *not* allow the fool to terrorize her or her family and teammates.

She sprinted to Quiy S<u>k</u>et's corral, seized his bridle, tossed her saddle on, strapped her pack onto her back, jumped up on the stud like she was the last one on in a race, and dashed off.

Jack stood leaning against his open cabin door with his arms folded and watched her gallop off. *A plan indeed.* He walked over and sat on his porch steps, taking a moment to pray for his friend. Nothing good could come about with the rage and revenge she har bored. "God help her," he whispered.

While Spupaleena was gone, Phillip circled up the remaining racers and finished his roster; there were only two teams he was missing. Pekam and the other teammates helped him complete the list after several attempts at the language barriers. He figured Spupaleena had enough troubles on her shoulders and was too full of pride to ask his wife for assistance. He was bound and determined to do it himself—he and the racers.

>**Incheechun's** ("Wolf") **teammates**:
>Rain drops—orange
>N haneekin – Beetle
>Stoonhuh – Beaver
>Chy-ha – Crawdad
>Sinkaleep – Coyote
>**Cheelkst Kawup** ("Five Horses") **teammates**:
>Grizzly paw—brown
>Swa – Cougar
>Simhaykin – Grizzly
>Wha Welwho – Fox
>Spokalitz – Ling

When Phillip was finished, he thanked the teams and shot off to find his wife. He was sure she would be impressed. A smile graced his face as he strutted down the path separating the pit-homes, greeting everyone as he strode by.

Chapter 10

It was settled.

The following morning, Spupaleena walked briskly up to her teammates. "Gather your stuff, we're going to the mountains to train. Get a week's worth of supplies. We need a pack horse or two." She scooped up horse blankets, halters, bridles, whips, and saddles and shoved them into her packs, barely glancing their way.

Ta <u>huh</u>t Skumhist and Hun han neekun flashed each other a quizzical look. <u>K</u>oo<u>k</u>yuma In-tee-tee-<u>huh</u> shrugged his shoulders and Chy chy pum Sn'e shook his head, giving Spupaleena a look of disgust.

"Where've *you* been?" Ta <u>huh</u>t Skumhist finally asked in a tone lathered in exasperation. "You just take off, not telling any of us. Then you come back and bark commands at us like we're your dogs?" Her brows shot up and she moved a couple steps closer to Spupaleena.

Spupaleena jerked her head up, glancing around from face to face. She saw the hurt in their eyes.

Spupaleena sighed, realizing what she had just done. There were no excuses. Coming back and shouting orders at everyone, her most trusted friends, and not even saying, "Hello and how is everyone?" was unacceptable.

Spupaleena dropped her pack and faced them all. "I'm sorry. I should've explained myself." She stepped closer to the group, wringing her hands. "I went across the river to Jack Dalley's place to get"—she glanced in the roan's direction—"Quiy S<u>k</u>et."

"I knew it!" Chy chy pum Sn'e snorted. He had never actually seen the giant, only heard the stories. Oh, how he wanted to touch, no smell the beast. His eyes were bulging and he was as excited as a squirrel that landed the last pine nut for the winter.

He started to walk toward Quiy S<u>k</u>et and Spupaleena grabbed his shirt sleeve. "Loot. You have packing to do. I'll introduce you all to him once we find camp."

"*Why* do we have to go to the mountains?" <u>K</u>oo<u>k</u>yuma In-tee-tee-<u>huh</u> whined.

"It'll be fun!" Hun han neekun chimed in. The pair continued their banter as they walked away.

Chy chy pum Sn'e looked at her with disappointed eyes, but nodded.

"Go!" Spupaleena snarled.

The boy turned and went with the others to finish getting ready.

Spupaleena glanced down at the pack that lay on its side with the contents spilling out. She looked up to see Elizabeth strolling her way, humming a favorite hymn. Her blond hair let loose, curls flowing down her back.

"Phillip finished his roster." Elizabeth giggled, wiping away beads of sweat from her flush face.

"He did?" Spupaleena smiled. "I can't wait to see it…and eventually read it."

The girls laughed, knowing how much the roster meant to Phillip, but also seeing how excited he had been with it.

Elizabeth's gaze fell to the ground. "Going somewhere?"

"Kewa. We need to get away from the distractions around here. Somewhere the fool can't find us." Spupaleena twisted from side to side, stretching the tight muscles in her back.

Elizabeth nodded. She picked up a brush and slid it over Dusty's neck from across the corral poles. She continued humming and praying for her friend.

Spupaleena could feel those prayers. She knew exactly what Elizabeth was praying for. Guilt poked up and down her spine as she fought it off—at least tried to. She denied any allegations of running, nor was she seeking revenge. Merely going away to train where it was quiet.

The team needed time to refocus for the upcoming race and get the alternate horses ready. Even though the stand-in horses would be used for only a race or two, they had to put forth the effort and not settle with a shoddy attempt.

"When will you be back?"

Spupaleena let out a deep sigh. "No more than five days. That should give us plenty of time. If we can actually get our exchanges to be smooth, maybe sooner. It's the horses that need the practice, not so much the people." She chuckled at the thought of bounding off one wide-eyed mount and jumping up on another. They would surely have their work cut out for them.

K̲o̲o̲k̲yuma In-tee-tee-h̲u̲h̲ came rushing up to the ladies. He was out of breath and wound up. "I have——a—he's huge—and his muscles—like a rock!" He spoke in between gasps of air surging into his burning lungs.

Elizabeth and Spupaleena exchanged glances. A cross expression exploded on Spupaleena's face.

"Did you go over and see Quiy Sk̲et when I asked you not to?"

The young man, with his long hair sticking out in all directions bent over resting his hands on his knees, nodded enthusiastically. "I couldn't help it. I crept over when no one was looking. He's so…so…"

Spupaleena shook her head. "Go! Pack." She jabbed her finger in the direction of the others.

"Right. Kewa."

"There's plenty to do."

He stood searching the ground for the next clue.

Spupaleena threw her hands up in the air. "Go! Find Hun han neekun. She'll get you lined out."

K̲o̲o̲k̲yuma In-tee-tee-h̲u̲h̲ whipped around and took two steps, turned back and asked, "Where is she?"

Spupaleena dropped her shoulders and counted silently: *naux, aseel, kalth̲ese*. "Try over there." She pointed to the girl's pit-home.

Elizabeth grinned. "Nice counting. It helps…one, two, three!" She chuckled, shaking her head.

"I saw you do that with the children. It works, what can I say?"

Elizabeth nodded. "Speaking of children, I confronted Hannah about lying to you concerning the pony and saying we agreed to her racing."

"Oh? What did she say?"

"Not much. She didn't deny it. But we had to have our, "It's too dangerous for you," talk again."

Spupaleena held a horse halter in her hands, fingering the leather on it. "Do you think it's better to let her have a horse rather than going behind your back?"

Elizabeth thought for a moment. "I don't know. She needs to learn to abide by our rules."

Spupaleena nodded.

"I just don't want her to get hurt. She's so little and fragile. No, I think she needs to wait, perhaps prove herself a little more in the area of trust and obedience."

Spupaleena grinned at her friend. "Well, I will be praying about it with you. I understand both sides, trust me."

"Thank you. Believe me, this is no easy situation. She just so badly wants to be a mini-you." Elizabeth sighed.

"And that's bad?" Spupaleena teased.

Elizabeth hugged her friend. "Most of the time, no." They laughed.

"I'll talk to her about lying to me, if that's all right with you. I will also try and share with her why I race, and that maybe when she's older, we could talk more. That may help hold her off for a bit."

Elizabeth nodded. "It can't hurt. Well, what do you need help with? Phillip and I talked and we can stay until you get back. He's having such a good time with your father trapping and setting snares. They're teaching each other. Besides, this will give me more time with Smil<u>k</u>ameen to learn more about the herbs your people use. Oh, she's learning some English, too, by the way. She acts like she doesn't like it. I still haven't seen her crack a smile, but I think she might when I'm not looking. Not sure though."

"I've never seen a smile cross that woman's face." Spupaleena grinned. "Wait, you and Phillip are staying; how did you know I was leaving?" Spupaleena grabbed her braids and slid her slender fingers part way down her thick hair.

"We know you too well, my friend." Elizabeth's eyes glinted.

"Besides, you have more words to learn. This will give me more time to plan." Elizabeth grew suddenly quiet.

"What is it?" Spupaleena asked.

"Some of the other children want to learn to read so they can communicate better with Hannah. What do you think?"

Spupaleena gasped. "Kewa. That's such a good idea. But the ranch…"

"We won't be gone that long. Besides, this time of year, there isn't as much to do. The calves are all born and with their mothers so Jack told us to take as long as we needed and he had it all covered."

A pang of guilt swept over Spupaleena. "I should have been nice to Jack."

"What?"

Spupaleena shrugged her shoulders. "When I went to get the stud, I was short with him. Rude actually. I was in a hurry to get back." She sighed.

Elizabeth nodded. "I'm sure you two will work it out."

"I owe him an apology," Spupaleena frowned.

"You'll get your chance." Elizabeth put a gentle hand on Spupaleena's shoulder.

The women finished organizing and packing the goods nice and tight. The team met at the north end of the village and trekked off into the woods. They rode in silence, concentrating on each leg of the race and their individual duties of the next several weeks.

It was mid-morning and everyone was packed and ready. Apprehension hung in the air. Spupaleena could see it on her teammates faces, all but K̲ook̲yuma In-tee-tee-h̲uh, who had a smile plastered on his, probably hoping and dreaming of riding Quiy Sk̲et. Spupaleena wondered if the girls were afraid she would have a melt down and take off again; she had positively earned their distrust. She would have to speak with them later, asking for their forgiveness.

Elizabeth watched them go, disappearing into the trees like visions in the night. A look of worry crossed her face as she turned to go and check on her family.

Pekam saw Elizabeth bustling toward him, skirt swishing with each step. He caught her eye and held a hand up suggesting they talk.

"Have you seen my lth̲kickha?"

"Yeah, they just left. I thought you knew?" Elizabeth tilted her head.

"Loot. Do I ever know?"

"Oh." Elizabeth covered her mouth and laughed, not meaning to make Pekam feel bad. "You have a point."

Pekam laughed too. "Where'd they go?"

Elizabeth shrugged her shoulders and pointed behind her.

"Do you know for how long?"

"She thought a week or less."

Pekam gave her a quizzical look.

"Five days or less." Elizabeth felt bad for the boy.

He nodded. "Lim lumt."

"You're welcome. Let me know if I can be of any more help." She winked.

Pekam grinned. "I guess it's time to train." He shrugged his scrawny shoulders and his thick, dark eyebrows shot up.

Elizabeth cocked her head. "What horses do you have to ride?"

"A relative loaned us his."

"Good. I hope your training goes well, Pekam."

"Lim lumt. See you later." Pekam trotted off. His long, wiry body looked like a cattail dancing in the wind.

Hannah's round, emerald eyes stared at the shaggy, sorrel-and-white pony standing quietly in front of her. Everything inside told her to grab the rein the boy held out to her. Her brown hair was braided tightly. She wore flannel-lined pants under her skirt for added warmth on the chilled spring day. She peered at the other girls and smiled because they too had pants under their doeskin dresses, but theirs were made of animal skins. She wondered what that would feel like.

The spitfire glanced around to see if her father or mother were close by. She knew one of her auntie's relatives had put Delbert and Lillian down for a nap. They were out of the way. Lillian was too little to tattle, but surely Delbert would. He would be the first to toddle as fast as his chubby little legs could carry him straight to Papa for a ride on the *nony*, as he called them.

More kids gathered with their ponies. Girls and boys from the ages of five and up came gawking at the timid, fair-skinned girl. Hannah put her hand up. She so badly wanted to reach for that lead rope, and then quickly dropped it. She sighed, stomped her foot, and set her tiny hands on her tiny hips.

Obey my parents…ride like auntie. The horsey smell enticed her more than anything. The soft fluffy pony hair that was starting to shed; she could feel it without even touching one. Every nerve in her three-foot body twitched with anticipation. She had only ridden with an adult, never alone, and never on a pony. This was the moment she had dreamed of—prayed for.

Looking down at the tiny, white-and-black hooves gave her courage. She could hear them pounding the earth as they ran with the others. Her fingers moved back and forth as they hung by her sides. Her heart felt like it would beat right out of her chest.

She rubbed the green knitted hat on her head then swiftly grabbed the rope that was fastened to the little mare. The surrounding kids cheered and Hannah beamed as if she had just won the pony in a race. She squealed in glee as her body shook with exhilaration and anticipation—the kind that ate at a kid. She quickly scanned the area for any sign of her parents.

Grinning, she allowed a girl to help hoist her on the sorrel-and-white pony that was almost the same size as her. Her milk-white teeth glimmered in the sun. She leaned over and clutched the pony's neck and sunk her red cheeks into the warmth of the thick, rabbit-like hair.

The day was perfect.

Nothing could wreck her day, not even a pair of finger-pointing, red-faced parents and the worst of punishments.

Chapter 11

Things were not going as planned.

Spupaleena lay on the ground covered in mud. She rubbed her aching muscles, wishing she were home warming her freezing body by the fire and sipping hot rosehip tea. She looked up at the velvety fir trees surrounding her. She wanted to cry, but laughed instead. This was day three. Things should be going better than they were.

<u>Koo</u><u>k</u>yuma In-tee-tee-<u>huh</u> stood over her. He stared down at her with a hand out to help her up and a scowl on his face.

"I'm getting up," Spupaleena moaned. Her muscles told her to quit, but her will insisted that she take a few more stabs at the exchanges. Her timing was off and she knew it.

"I'm tired too, but we need this win."

Spupaleena rolled to her side and forced herself to stand up. "Kewa. Let's do it again."

She grabbed hold of Quiy S<u>k</u>et and led him to a stick they used as a starting point. Before she hopped up on the leggy roan, she leaned on him and prayed for strength and endurance. She took longer than normal to pray, buying time to catch her breath.

After a few stretches, and more than a few impatient looks from Kookyuma In-tee-tee-huh, she stood to the side of her horse, took a running step and slid across the roan's back. She laid there for a minute before sitting up.

Spupaleena stroked his neck. "Okay boy, here we go. Let's get this right, shall we?" She walked him several yards back, turned, and waited for the signal.

Kookyuma In-tee-tee-huh raised his arm as Hun han neekun struggled to hold her anxious horse still. He dropped it quickly and Spupaleena raced their way.

"Come on, nail this one." The boy eyed his teammate as she rode low and slightly forward, getting off the stallion's back. Her knees held tight to his sides as she moved in motion to his rhythm. The stallion took long, smooth strides that barely took him off the ground.

Spupaleena reined in Quiy Sket and as his hooves began to slow, she pushed away from the solid beast and slid off his back before Kookyuma In-tee-tee-huh had a firm grasp on the lead. She took a few steps as the momentum picked her up and placed her on the waiting horse's back. Hun han neekun swiftly stepped off to the side as the pair rushed off.

Kookyuma In-tee-tee-huh jumped up and down as he let out a piercing cry while the wind nabbed it and chased after them. "You did it!"

Spupaleena clenched her jaw as she fought to concentrate on the second and upcoming switch. As they neared the team, she could see Ta <u>huh</u>t Skumhist straining to hang on to the sorrel Overo stallion as he danced about impatiently. Chy chy pum Sn'e waved his arms in the air hollering the stout horse's name. The bay Tobiano pinned his eyes and ears on the familiar voice, dashing straight for him, trusting to be caught and rewarded with rest.

As the wet spring earth sprayed out beneath the heaving stallion, Spupaleena grabbed the rein and gently pulled back. The bay responded and slowed his feet. Spupaleena eyed the still dancing sorrel as she slid off, took three long, smooth steps and hopped up in the air. The sorrel Overo swung over, crashing his hip into Spupaleena's side and sent her flying. She screamed out in alarm as she sailed though the air.

"Loo—" Ta <u>huh</u>t Skumhist shrieked as she dropped the rein and ran for Spupaleena.

Chy chy pum Sn'e grabbed both stallions and followed closely behind. The horses led willingly and he was thankful for it, or so he thought. Before he knew it, the sorrel pulled back and was biting at the bay. The bay pawed the sorrel, striking him in the shoulder. Chy chy pum Sn'e shouted at the pair as if they were little kids bickering over a toy.

Neither listened.

Ta <u>huh</u>t Skumhist heard the commotion from behind as she watched Spupaleena hit the ground hard and roll like a pinecone in a windstorm. She stopped and turned and watched her friend being tussled around in the middle of a stud fight. She jerked her hands over her mouth, looking back at Spupaleena and made the decision to help Chy chy pum Sn'e.

Spupaleena groaned as she held her head in her hands and laid in a fetal position on the damp grass. She tried to focus on the commotion close by, but only saw a blurred figure running away. *Where are you going?* she thought as her mind slipped away in a deep fog.

Ta <u>huh</u>t Skumhist made her way close enough to the scrapping horses as she dare without putting herself in danger. She reached out and tried to grab a rein but missed. She attempted a second and third time and failed. She clenched her jaw and set her feet as her gaze locked on the closest rein. She held out her hand and mirrored the swinging hunk of rope until it came into reach and she latched on.

She stepped to the side, disengaging the bay's hind end and moved him out of the sorrel's way. Chy chy pum Sn'e clutched the sorrel's rein and circled him to the trees. He secured the stud to a sturdy pine tree and ran for Spupaleena. Ta <u>huh</u>t Skumhist did the same. The horses settled down and went to munching on last summer's yellow grass.

Chy chy pum Sn'e knelt beside Spupaleena as she lay on the ground catching her breath. "Are you hurt?" He looked at her with his hands in the air afraid to touch anything that would cause pain.

"Is she hurt?" Ta <u>huh</u>t Skumhist said as she slid to her friend's side.

"I don't know. She hasn't said anything."

"Spupaleena, are you hurt?"

Chy chy pum Sn'e looked at Ta <u>huh</u>t Skumhist and frowned. "I already asked that."

"I know and you said she didn't answer. I'm asking again you big...big..." She sighed, shaking her head and slumped over Spupaleena.

"I'm fine, really." Spupaleena slurred, their loud voices booming in her head.

The teammates exchanged frightened glances.

"You're hurt again—I mean your head—you're hurt." Ta <u>huh</u>t Skumhist placed a tender hand on Spupaleena's arm. She lifted her eyes to Chy chy pum Sn'e. "I overheard Elizabeth telling her father that one more injury to the head would do permanent damage."

Chy chy pum Sn'e's eyes grew round. He peered down at Spupaleena who was staring up at him.

"I just got the wind knocked out of me. I'm fine. I didn't even hit my head." Spupaleena rolled onto her back and shut her eyes. "I just need a minute, and I think we're done for the day. We'll start fresh in the morning."

Chy chy pum Sn'e just stared at her.

Ta <u>huh</u>t Skumhist sat back on her heels and pursed her lips. "Well then, what do we do now? We can't just sit here in the cold, wet dirt."

"Just give me a minute." Spupaleena covered her eyes with her arm, blocking out the rays that were fighting its way through the dark, rolling clouds, stinging her pupils.

"I'm going to get Big Red and head back to the others. Meet you guys back at camp," Ta <u>huh</u>t Skumhist blurted out.

"I guess I'll stay with you," Chy chy pum Sn'e said as he glanced around, unsure of what to do.

Ta <u>huh</u>t Skumhist stood and turned to walk off. She glanced back, seemingly agitated, and spoke before retrieving the roan, "Don't take too long, I'm sure you need to eat or something."

Spupaleena snorted. *That one needs a load of patience.*

The next morning, Spupaleena woke to a hushed argument. She strained to hear but couldn't make sense of it. She could tell it was the girls talking, but couldn't fathom what they would be squabbling over. She lay motionless with her eyes closed. Still she could not make out the words.

"What's the problem?" She yelled out.

The voices went silent.

Spupaleena snickered to herself. The girls seemed to bicker over the most mindless, made-up problems.

"What's going on?" She bit her lip, holding back a giggle as she tried to sound tough.

The girls crawled into the make-shift tent and sat beside Spupaleena, who looked from girl to girl with her dark eyebrows raised.

The girls glanced at one another. Ta <u>huh</u>t Skumhist scowled, while Hun han neekun looked down sheepishly.

"What is it this time? Did one of the boys unlace and hide your moccasins?" Spupaleena asked as she tried to keep a somber face.

"Loot,"—Ta <u>huh</u>t Skumhist said as she glared down at Spupaleena—"they did not. Whiny here thinks we need to take you back home so the grumpy healer can look at your mushy head."

A red hue, the color of Indian Paint Brush, crept up Hun han neekun's neck. "Kewa, I think you should—maybe Elizabeth could—"

"Oh, spit it out, softy." Ta <u>huh</u>t Skumhist rolled her eyes and made some guttural sound deep in the back of her throat.

"I just think—well, I overheard Elizabeth say that you could be seriously hurt if your head hit the ground again. Chy chy pum Sn'e said you took a pretty bad fall, and well—I just think we should take you back to get looked at." Hun han neekun tried out her most brave voice.

"As twisted with words as you are, how do you hold those big, powerful horses?" Ta <u>huh</u>t Skumhist scoffed.

Hun han neekun pursed her lips and kept her eyes fixed on Spupaleena, who sat and smiled brightly at the two quarreling girls. What opposites they were, but she was glad nonetheless, they were both on her team. Spupaleena found one of her greatest pleasures in watching their strong-as-ox power as they hung on to those dancing horses when she came in for the transfer. Even though both girls were night and day, they were the same strong women when it counted—helping the team to do their best. Yes, she was honored to have them.

"So, what now?" Han hun neekun said raising a questioning brow.

"I think I'm ready for a couple more days of this, aren't you?" Spupaleena insisted. Hun han neekun grunted, giving her a scornful gaze.

"Look, I didn't hit my head. I merely got the wind knocked out of me. I have a few bruises. I'm sore, but that's all. Really."

Ta huht Skumhist clapped her hands together. "Good, then get ready and let's head out."

"I'm hungry and want to grab a quick bite to eat, and then we'll go." Spupaleena peered at Hun han neekun. "Lim lumt for being so concerned about me. I promise to be careful and not tire myself out like yesterday. We'll take longer breaks in between sets and take more time to settle the horses."

Hun han neekun nodded. "It's your stubbornness that allows you to win. You know that, right?" She took some dried salmon out of her pack and tossed it to Spupaleena.

Spupaleena chuckled. "Kewa, I do. I also realize if we do this only part way, someone *will* get seriously hurt, and I won't allow that to happen. Your safety is too important, more than any race."

"Enough of this soft talk—hurry up. I'll go get the horses ready and meet you outside." Ta huht Skumhist grunted and crawled out the tent. "I hate girl talk," she grumbled. "I just want to practice."

"If you want, you can have some mantalk with us," Kookyuma In-tee-tee-huh teased as she walked past him with a scowl on her face.

Ta huht Skumhist stopped. She pursed her lips and clenched her fists.

Chy chy pum Sn'e burst out laughing, then covered his mouth, half afraid of her sporadic wrath.

"If I wanted to talk to you two ***oo pa weekin*** ("Stink Bugs"), I would have." She turned on her heels and strode off. The boys laughed and watched her short, choppy strides make her tight, waist-long braids bob up and down. They exchanged glances and laughed some more, acting like they were fist fighting.

It was not long before Spupaleena crawled out from her tent with a huge smile, ready to start the day. She reached high into the air stretching her stiff muscles, and then she touched her palms to the ground as blood rushed to her head. She stood straight and hopped up and down so her crimson, liquid life would pump through her veins giving her energy and oxygen. Two necessities she would be counting on to get her through the day.

She sauntered over to her teammates and horses, watching them finish tacking up the horses. She giggled at their playfulness. Grabbing a brush, she quickly groomed Quiy Sket and tossed a saddle over his back. She cinched him up snug and made him trot a few circles to loosen any stiff muscles and gain his attention.

Chy chy pum Sn'e grabbed one of Ta huht Skumhist's braids, while Kookyuma In-tee-tee-huh snatched up the other. They played like they were pulling in opposite directions. By the grim look on Ta huht Skumhist's face, she was none too amused.

Hun han neekun quietly finished saddling up the borrowed horse, but her mind was on Spaoos Newt, hoping the boys were too busy teasing her friend and wouldn't notice her dreamy behavior. She wished he had been well enough to bring along. Seeing the big bay in her mind, she knew why his name meant Heart Breaker. He was stout and beautiful and gentle. He had the brightest, bluest eyes she'd ever seen. He surely broke the hearts of those who secretly wished they owned him—including her.

"Look who's pretending to be so busy at work over here." K̲oo̲k̲yuma In-tee-tee-h̲u̲h̲ started in Hun han neekun's direction, but feeling sorry for the meek girl, Spupaleena cut him off.

"About ready?"

Hun han neekun caught Spupaleena's gaze and thanked her silently. Spupaleena smiled and nodded.

K̲oo̲k̲yuma In-tee-tee-h̲u̲h̲ frowned and kicked at the dirt with his moccasin-covered toe. He was looking forward to a little ribbing. Hun han neekun was much more fun to tease because she was a better sport and would tease back, although he never really minded pulling punches at Ta h̲u̲h̲t Skumhist who usually started most of the taunting.

Spupaleena grabbed Quiy Sk̲et and jumped on. She took a couple minutes to lie on his back and rub him all over. He melted in her hands as they both relaxed into the rhythmic massage.

K̲oo̲k̲yuma In-tee-tee-h̲u̲h̲ and Hun han neekun hopped up on one horse, warmed him up, and trotted down a half-mile, grassy lane to their exchange site. Ta h̲u̲h̲t Skumhist and Chy chy pum Sn'e mounted the second horse, riding a mile to their transfer site.

Spupaleena took her time softening Quiy Sk̲et's body and catching his attention by starting and stopping him at a walk, trot, and canter. She would save the gallop for later. She hopped off and on his back a few times and then just jumped up and down at his side. She waited for him to lower his head, cock a hind leg, or sigh. She watched for the slightest sign that he was beginning to relax and then quietly stood beside him. Talking to him tenderly, she rubbed from his neck to his hind end, rewarding his effort. Spupaleena smiled. He stood so patiently and was so well mannered. How could someone so mean and evil have ever owned such a glorious creature? She silently thanked God for bringing him to her.

They did the same routine for awhile knowing it would take time for the others to arrive at their positions and settle in for the practice run. She stole a moment to close her eyes and began singing her lullaby in the peacefulness of the afternoon. "Running in the field, so happy and free, a black pony, a blue pony, a green pony. Kewa, three." Spupaleena took that time to just enjoy and bond with her glorious, red token of victory.

Chapter 12

A red-tailed hawk screeched overhead as if to say, "Stop! Don't do it." Hannah looked up from the top of the pony with those green, pleasing eyes of hers and watched the magnificent bird soar on a wind current, dive a few yards, and flap its outstretched wings as he raced toward the brilliant blue sky. Oh, how she dreamed of floating and soaring and racing with the wind as it slapped her in the face while she sailed up high in the air, seeing the tops of trees and the fish swimming and jumping in the Columbia River.

She smiled as she shaded her eyes with her chubby, little hand, staring and dreaming. She giggled and waved as if the bird was showing off just for her. She was an audience of one; just her and the hawk.

"Are you coming?" A boy's voice said, shaking her out of the trance.

Hannah pulled her focus away from the twirling bird to the pudgy boy and nodded. "Kewa, I'm coming," she said softly, sighing and wishing she could stay for just a little longer. She snuck one last peek and then turned, kicking her pony into a bumpy, little trot.

A smile plastered her face as she bounced along behind the rest of the group. What a joyous day, soaring with a free-spirited hawk and riding a painted pony by herself. Things could not get any better—even if she was the last one to cross the finish line—this day was still the best day of her life.

"Raise your hand if you're racing," a boy with a gruff voice spouted in the Sinyekst tongue. He sat on top of a little gray pony as plump as he was. The gelding stood quiet, stiff looking. His eyes were half closed as if he could just lay down into a deep sleep dreaming about lush, green grass by a nice cool creek. Hannah stared at the gray as if she was wondering whether the boy just plumb rode the pony to death or if he was just fat and sluggish.

Most of twenty kids waved their hands in the air, pleading with the boy to be one of the first to line up. He was obviously the leader of the pack. He searched the crowd in a superior-like manner deciding what group of hungry competitors should go first.

With that much noise, Hannah scanned the area to see how far they were from the village. If her parents found out…

"Hey, you racing or not?" Hannah looked his way and noticed that the boy was pointing at her. She blushed and shyly nodded.

A frantic feeling suddenly caught her breath, and her tummy started to fill with butterflies. She scanned the area and saw the village through the scattered pine trees. Looking ahead to where the race would start, she guessed they would eventually end up around the rocky face of a shorter hill that was actually tall enough to hide the finish line.

That torn feeling was back, the one that made a person know what they were about to do was wrong, even sinful. The kind of feeling that if her mother and father found out there would be big trouble. But still, mama and papa supported and loved to watch Auntie Spuppy ride, race, and win. Well, win most of the time. Yet, they did cheer her on. *How could they be mad if I did win*, she thought.

Hannah nodded with a newfound confidence. She had just talked herself into racing and of course, winning, even if this was her first day of riding by herself. It was in her genes. It had to be. Spuppy was her auntie after all.

A teeth baring smile crossed the girl's face as she lifted her tiny hand in the air and waved it as if this was her one and only chance to prove her bigness; that her parents could look at her as a serious pony rider. Maybe then they would even get her a pony to call her own. She would have to think of names. But first, she had a race to win.

"You, you, and you. Kewa, all of you in the back. Kewa, with the fat, grumpy-looking pony, come up to the start line." The same scraggly leader, who looked to be about eight-years-old or so, hollered at the oldest-looking children and waved them over. He sat on his gray pony, slumped over like the others were wasting his time. His pony was dirty and lazy and so was his owner. The boy was obviously not a racer, just the self-proclaimed director—the one with the most important roll, at least in his own mind.

"Hey, what about us?" A scrappy looking girl, who seemed to be about six-years-old, held her arms out, palms up. She wore a tattered doeskin dress with most of the fringe missing. Her braids were nice and neat and her moccasins looked newly sewn, a size too big and lined with fresh rabbit pelts. Her nose was bright red under her squinty eyes and arched brow.

Hannah struggled to know what they said with words, but between body babble and facial chatter she knew their meaning. She nodded in support of the girl. "Kewa, when *do* we get to ride?"

Everyone quickly turned to look at her. She felt like shrinking in her miniature saddle, but instead sat with her shoulders straight and proud just as she had seen her auntie do. She gazed at the boy, trembling like a frightened puppy, but nevertheless held her stance.

The boy simply shrugged. He turned to the girl and simply said, "Soon." The girl looked at Hannah and smiled. Hannah shrugged her shoulders and decided to work with the pony as she had watched Spupaleena work with Dusty and **Nee Ap Kukneeya** ("Forever Listening"), the horse Spupaleena had won last spring with a reckless boy who thought he was prepared to race. The poor Appaloosa failed to perform and was sold at the Kettle Falls to a trapper from some little town in northern Idaho. Hannah never did like that horse. He was a dirty spotted color and ugly to look at.

Hannah took hold of the looped, horsehair rein and began to turn the pony in circles, first one way and then the other. She walked the midget of a mare forward, stopped and tried to back her with mouth-rooting resistance. The stubborn pony planted those hooves of hers and refused to take a step back. Hannah was at a loss. She inadvertently began to hum and decided to just keep circling the pony. She pulled her around a few trees and wild rosebushes and jumped a couple of downed, rotted larch limbs the diameter of a ground hog.

She looked up to see the nice girl close by, watching her every move. Hannah smiled, but refrained from waving. She wanted to, but the girl's scowl caused her to lose her nerve. Hannah felt alone. She wanted to be the girl's friend, but without being able to really speak the Sinyekst language, the barrier was too great. It was a hard, guttural language. Hannah tried to learn words, knowing only a few easy ones like yes, no, and thank you. She would rather the kids learn English where the words and sounds were simple.

She looked up again and saw that the nice girl was still watching her. Hannah glanced down quickly, anticipating the look on her face would be the same. She decided to sneak a second peek and this time what she saw on the scrappy looking girl's face was actually a smile. It was small but still a smile.

Hannah beamed inside as her hopes of a new friend gathered and warmed her pounding heart. She worked her pony out of sheer joy and a spark of hope she just knew would soon ignite into a budding new friendship. Her smile grew at the thought of them riding together, playing and swimming once the weather turned warm.

She could see them giggling by the river, tossing rocks into the slow-moving current, and searching for turtles and other small creatures.

In her own little world of pleasant dreaming, Hannah heard a voice and glanced up to see the nice girl waving her over. The first round of older children had finished and the winner proudly trotted his pony in front of the onlookers, blurting out what she assumed was victorious jargon. Wisps of stray hair from his long ponytail twisted as it hung back from the wild and bouncy ride.

The gruff boy waved the younger lot over and they lined up their fidgety ponies in a jagged-looking row. He yelled out the rules in a low-pitched, snippy voice and held up a pudgy hand clutching a thin, sparse pine branch.

Hannah looked at that pine branch with wonder. She shrugged her shoulders and fixed her eyes on a wild rosebush straight ahead, just past the turn that would take her to the finish line, or rope. She hoped it would be a rope because her auntie sped through one when she raced.

Hannah glanced around not knowing what to expect. Her nerves fluttered as she eyed the other kids. She had never raced before and after all, this was the first day she had ridden a horse, big or small, by herself. She saw the nice girl working her chestnut pony, keeping his nose pointed forward. Hannah's pony just stood there and all the sudden, Hannah was scared. Scared she would fall off. Scared the pony wouldn't know what to do or do nothing at all. Scared she would turn around and her mother and father would be glaring at them, yanking her off, and forcing her to go back to the village.

The boy jerked the sparse-looking pine branch toward the ground as he yelled something she couldn't understand. The ponies darted away. Hannah's little black-and-white sped off nearly knocking her to the ground. She clung to the miniature saddle horn as if her life depended on it. She accidently let loose of the rein and was too terrified to reach out and try to grab it. She forgot about using the rosebush as a focal point, but no matter because her pony stuck with the herd.

As they were rounding the bend, she noticed her little black-and-white was not far behind and gaining speed. A picture of a courageous Auntie Spupaleena flashed in her mind and Hannah glanced at the horsehair loop thumping the pony's neck and thick brown mane. She looked up and back at the bouncing rein. She mustered her nerve and snapped at it and missed. She clung to the saddle horn and a grimace crossed her face. She was now mad at herself for not being as tough as her auntie was.

The finish rope was just ahead and she was now somewhere in the middle of the pack. She had to grab hold of that irritating rein before she crossed the rope. She stared at it for a few bouncy strides and then reached out. A jerk in the stride made her lose her gaze, but she felt its softness in her hand and without thinking, her chubby, little fingers closed around that braided rein.

Her eyes grew round and a smile lit up her face. "Yaaay," she screeched as she bounced up and down on the back of her wide-eyed pony. It didn't matter if she won or lost. She was just happy that she had raced, stayed on, and finished. She clapped her hands as her eyes went in pursuit of the nice girl.

"Hannah Marie Gardner!" A muffled call floated through the air.

Hannah heard a voice. Her name. She searched the area, but saw nothing.

"Hannah, over here."

The girl looked past the gruff boy and saw her parents rushing toward her, their faces crossed with concern. Her nightmare had just begun.

Hannah swallowed and slowly walked the black-and-white their way. Her chin dropped to her chest as a pit in her belly quickly formed. Her lashes cast upward as she made her way toward her parents. Earlier she was certain angry parents could not ruin her day. Now she was sure they could.

Chapter 13

The fool paced his pit-home, ranting about his next move. His face was ablaze with rage and hatred. He pumped his fists as his teammates sat motionless hoping his fiery temper would snuff out quickly. Words and thoughts rambled on lacking any trace of logic.

The mid-April morning was cool and damp. Hahoola<u>who</u>'s pit home was the opposite, searing and thick with emotion. Heat steaming out from the fool's sweat-covered flesh smelled as rancid as a ripe skunk.

"How could they have saved those horses? We gave them enough poison to kill ten more." The fool shook his fist in the air. "We need to make sure that girl never rides again."

Toople slowly nodded, smiling so big his eyes were mere slits. Swas kee's whole body bounced up and down with the jerky nod of his head. He glanced around to see the other's reaction; he was sure they were all in agreement.

Pelpalwheechula and Ska ka ka exchanged glances and shook their heads. Pelpalwheechula rolled her eyes and tossed a twig into the orange coals. Ska ka ka stood tall and stepped in front of Hahoola<u>who</u>.

He held his hands out to the leader. "I will *not* be a part of this."

The fool sneered at his disloyal teammate.

Ska ka ka stared deep into the fool's gaze, not cowering one bit. "I came to ride. I'm finished here. This is your battle, not mine." Ska ka ka turned and walked out. He did not hesitate. He did not turn for one last glance. He strode forward, tall and sure, looking ahead to his future. He was certain he could muster up three riders who were serious competitors.

Hahoola<u>who</u> spit on the ground. "We don't need him," he growled. "There are plenty of men who would love to ride with me. I'll have one by the end of the day."

"Two." Pelpalwheechula stood and stared at the fool.

"What?"

"Two. You need to find *two* people who will ride with the likes of you. I'm with Ska ka ka. I came to race, not worry about your petty ego. You're just mad that Spupaleena beat you and took your horse as her prize."

Hahoola<u>who</u> raised a fist to her and she stood her ground. He jerked a finger and spewed insults at her, but she laughed it off and went in search of Ska ka ka. She would rather ride with someone bold enough to stand up for his passion than a yellow-bellied bully who was stupid enough to lose his own horse to his enemy. Fool indeed.

"Ska ka ka—wait—I want to talk to you," Pelpalwheechula hollered in between steps littered with pinecones and sticks.

Ska ka ka turned around and looked at her, amazed and a little dumfounded. The fringe on her dress twitched in all directions as she made her way to his side. She stopped, bent over and pulled up her knee-high moccasin, and then grabbed his arm.

"Let's make a team. With the both of us, we only need two more riders. We can easily find a couple more people good enough to pull this off with little practice."

Ska ka ka shook his head. "I don't know."

"We can do this. I know we can."

The boy stood and thought a moment. "Who? Do you have someone all ready picked out?"

"I thought you might since you walked out on Hahoola<u>who</u>."

Ska ka ka laughed. "No, I don't. I just refuse to ride with a person who has nothing but settling a score on his mind."

"I feel the same way. I've worked too hard to be stuck with someone so evil."

There was a moment of silence.

"Three."

"What?" Pelpalwheechula turned to Ska ka ka and laughed. "Three?"

"Yes, we need three more people. Remember, one rider and two exchange teams of two."

Pelpalwheechula giggled. "You're right. I know people. I'll go now and do some fast talking."

Ska ka ka smiled down at her. He had never heard her giggle before. He saw her as someone who would rather scrap with the boys than play dolls with the girls.

They walked in silence until Pelpalwheechula chuckled. "I can't wait to see his reaction when he sees the girl racing his—the roan."

His brows shot up. "What? She has Quiy S<u>k</u>et?"

"Uh huh." She snickered.

Ska ka ka slapped his leg and roared with laughter. He motioned his friend to follow along. Together they would find the perfect trio to join their new team, with strong colors and an honorable symbol to ride proudly on the rump of their horses. Horses. Now they would need horses. He sighed and prayed the Creator would provide him with strong, fast horses.

"What do you think you're doing, young lady?" Elizabeth's eyes bulged and her finger pointing was a weapon to be feared. Phillip was right behind her. The scowl on his face was just as scary to Hannah. She silently prayed that God would not let her parents explode in their anger.

Her long brown eyelashes faced the ground and her emerald eyes begged to peek out from under them, but the little spitfire was afraid to see the steam she feared rose from her fuming parents' ears. All of the sudden, she didn't feel very brave. She felt like sneaking off the pony and crawling under a rock.

Elizabeth and Phillip stopped in front of her and just stood, staring. It was as irritating as smoke in her eyes—maybe even worse. It was not only irritating, it was just plain frightening. Hannah wondered if they would speak first or if she should. She started to squirm. She was still worried about looking her parents in the face.

Finally she spoke. "I'm sorry," she said, barely audible.

Phillip smiled and Elizabeth turned to peer at him. She gave him a look that said, *stop it now or pay the penalty.* Phillip knew his daughter had not seen him. Her pouty lip was just too precious. But yes, she was certainly in trouble and would have consequences. He realized that and not by the harsh look on his wife's face.

Phillip nodded to Elizabeth and turned his face to the yes-you-are-in-trouble look and went back to staring at his darling little bundle. He gazed at her all dressed warm and snug. She wore the green hat her mother had tenderly knit for her over the winter. His baby girl's round emerald eyes, wet with promising tears, tugged at his heart strings. Again he recognized the seriousness of her offense and fought off the precious-little-bundle thoughts and became serious again. *Lord, help me,* he thought.

"What are you doing here, missy?" Elizabeth raked her fingers through her blond locks. She set her hands on her petite waist, making herself look taller than she really was.

"I—I went riding, then I was talked into racing this pony with the others." She finally decided to be brave and look her mother in the eyes. She glanced around for support from someone—the nice girl—anyone.

"Were you forced to jump in that saddle and ride?"

"No, Mama."

"Were you forced to race that little pony with the others?"

Hannah looked sheepishly at her mother, and then at her father who gave her a small smile, and then back at her mother.

She shook her head. "No, Mama," she whispered

"You did this without our permission." Phillip said matter-of-factly. He thought he better chime in and support his wife.

"Yes, Papa. I did." Hannah gazed at the ground. Shame engulfed her little body.

"What made you disobey us?" Elizabeth asked, arching her brows.

"I just…I just wanted to ride like Auntie Spuppy. I'm sorry." Hannah sighed. She reached down and patted the black-and-white, figuring it might be the last time she would be able to touch the pony's bunny-soft hair. Tears trickled down her cheeks. "I won't do it again. I promise." She whispered.

Phillip and Elizabeth exchanged sad-looking glances. Their hearts sank.

"I know you're sorry," Elizabeth gave her a stern look, "but how do we know you'll never do this again? And without our knowing?" Spupaleena's words popped into her mind, *Do you want her to ride behind your back?* She shuddered.

Hannah thought for a moment. "I'll ask you and if you say no, then I won't ride—ever again." Her voice trailed off in a mournful ending.

Phillip sucked in a breath, stifling a laugh. Elizabeth reached back and jabbed him in the ribs with her elbow. Phillip moaned, rubbing his side. Hannah glanced down wearing the most pitiful expression on her face. Phillip smiled; he could do that with no threat of pain from his wife's body parts.

"You *will* have extra chores to do for your punishment," Elizabeth jabbed her finger at her daughter. "You know that, right?"

"Yes, Mama."

"Where did you get this horse?" Phillip asked. He examined the remaining gawkers for a hint of ownership. There were no takers.

Hannah shrugged her shoulders. "A boy handed me the reins and," Hannah glanced around spotting the nice girl and pointed in her direction, "she helped me on." Her expression lightened enough to at least locate the girl. She searched the few riders that were left, but the boy was nowhere to be found.

Phillip took off his Stetson and wiped his face with his shirt sleeve, not that he was sweating but more out of a nervous habit. "Well, I guess you better find the owner of that pony. Do you think the girl over there will help you?" Phillip gestured to the nice girl.

Hannah nodded.

Phillip turned to his serious, little wife. "I'll go ask Skumhist if he has any idea."

Elizabeth nodded and watched her husband walk off.

"Mama," Hannah said, "did you watch me ride?"

Elizabeth turned her attention back to her daughter and smiled. "Yes, dear, I did."

"Did I ride like Auntie Spuppy?"

Elizabeth giggled. "Yes, yes, you did." She could not lie.

Hannah beamed and sat taller in that miniature saddle on that miniature black-and-white horse.

"Come on now. Let's go and see if we can find an owner for her and then you can talk to Pekam."

"Why Uncle Pekam?" Hannah arched one small, brown brow.

"Because, he knows all about repentance work, believe me." Elizabeth laughed.

"What's pen-ants work, Mama?"

"Ask Uncle Pekam. He'll tell ya." Elizabeth snickered, grabbing hold of the rein and led the miniature pair towards the nice girl who examined them both—closely.

Chapter 14

The April's showers finally gave way to May's sunnier days. The morning was warm. Wisps of clouds hung high in the deep blue sky and the air was still and smelled clean from the previous day's drizzling rain. The earth was damp, but everyone's spirits were festive.

Today's race was held to the land east of the Kettle Falls and two teams from neighboring Native villages decided to join them. Word had it that these teams were coming to win. They were strong, all young men, and as fierce as an angry cougar. One team, from the *Spukanee* people, came from a southeastern territory, north of Spokane. Phillip had seen these people fishing in the Spokane River on occasion while trapping. English trappers called them: The Children of the Sun.

The other team came from the east, along the Pend Oreille River. French trappers referred to them as the river paddlers, but they called themselves, *Kalispeliwho*—The Brown Camas People.

The trees were deep green and glinted as the sun's rays brushed against the needles. The grass poked its head up from under the rich, black earth, peeking under last year's dried-out meadow and smelled fresh and seasoned. The wild lilies were in full bloom and their sweet aroma wafted in the gentle breeze.

Spupaleena emerged from the tipi her father set up for them and filled her lungs with the fresh pine and wildflower scents surrounding her. She smiled brightly and lifted her face to the warm, bright sun. They used the temporary homes made of tule-mats that were woven together since they would be in the area for a week or more. Skumhist figured they would stay and fish since the family was so close to the falls.

She looked around, gazing at the purple and yellow wildflowers that had already bloomed, and the ones still stretching out of their buds. She had never really examined them, let alone appreciated their beauty—until now. She strolled over to a patch of wild lilies and observed the yellow petals peeking through their protective covers. A purple crocus caught her attention and she knelt to finger its delicate petals.

"Spupaleena," Pekam called out to her. He pressed his fingers to the side of his face and groaned. He stood, glaring at her.

She sighed, tilting her head to observe the flowers, turning to the sound of his low pitched voice. Waving, she turned for one last glance, and then strode toward her brother.

"What were you doing?" His tone sounded sharp.

"Looking at the flowers. Why?"

Pekam rubbed the back of his neck. He turned as if searching for the right meaning. "Nothing. It's just… why? I don't know. You never have before."

"So, what's wrong with it?" Spupaleena could feel the tension leave her body as her thoughts wandered to the purple crocus.

Pekam shrugged his shoulders. "Nothing"—Pekam shook his head in wonder and stood, trying to remember what he came to see her about—"I said nothing."

Spupaleena grabbed her braids and shifted her weight as she stood. Waiting.

"Guess what?" Spupaleena asked.

"What? We have a race and you feel like…like… smelling flowers and playing games?"

"Loot. But really, guess." Pekam fidgeted like an ignored puppy wanting to play.

"Your saddle broke and you get to ride bareback, your dream has come true."

Pekam stood still and tossed his sister a disgusted look. He struggled to figure out why she was acting so strangely.

Spupaleena shrugged. She felt like she was seeing the beauty of the landscape for the first time.

"Guess who's not here and doesn't have a team." Pekam whispered, leaning close to Spupaleena like the news was top secret.

"Incheechun?"

Pekam stood straight and flicked his finger on her nose.

"Ouch! What'd you do that for?"

"A brainless answer deserves a brainless response." Pekam smirked.

Spupaleena giggled, rubbing the end of her nose as water formed in her eyes from the sting of his thumb and finger.

"Okaaay. Who then?" Spupaleena shook her head, attempting to fling the sting to the ground.

"The fool." Pekam spoke slowly and softly.

"What? Where is he?" Spupaleena grunted. "Probably hiding under a rock waiting for his lap dog, Swas Kee, to say the coast is clear."

They both chuckled.

"Loot, lthkickha. I heard Ska ka ka and Pelpalwheechula walked out on him. They were tired of his raging outbursts and left." Pekam's eyes glinted in the morning sun. A small smile crossed his face. "Nobody will ride with him, so he doesn't have a team."

Pekam laughed at his sister who stood open mouthed and wordless.

Spupaleena shook her head; her thoughts were a blur. "I can't believe this. What a fool." The corners of her mouth curved up, then quickly pursed and the twinkle in her eyes was replaced with dark clouds as her thoughts turned to the poisoning of her horses. She was still convinced the fool was behind it all.

"Kewa, the name you gave him is a good match, like me and Seech Sneewt." Pekam twirled around like a chicken on fire, whooping and howling with his nose pointed to the ground.

Spupaleena watched her brother and a snicker turned into a chuckle until a hearty giggle escaped her lips. She clapped her hands and laughed, deep in her belly—the only involuntary reaction her dazed body could make. She laughed until tears poured out of her glossy, black eyes and her belly ached so bad she doubled over. Pekam kept on dancing and clucking, making silly noises and animal-like movements.

After a time, she was able to pull herself together and suddenly, and unexpectedly, sadness showered her like rain. She wanted to beat him—badly. And now her chance was snuffed out.

Pekam stopped laughing and stared at her sudden gloomy appearance. "What's wrong?"

"I—I just wanted to race him again, and beat him, beat him good." Spupaleena's gaze fixed on the ground. She crossed her arms in front of her and a frown overtook her mouth.

"Lthkickha…" Pekam was at a loss for words. All their excitement had been doused with one quick, depressing, ugly thought. He rolled a pinecone around with his wet, moccasin-covered toe. If he had pockets in his breeches, like the ones Phillip had in his pants, he would have slid his hands in them. Now he knew why Phillip did it. The feelings flooding him at that moment were awkward. He hated to see his self-assured sister so out of sorts. Disappointed. Crushed.

He struggled to even describe the pit in his stomach. His heart ached and his spirits dropped like a rock in the water. The ripples of discontent spread as his joyous mood disappeared. He too had a strong desire to annihilate the fool in this race. His first chance and now that was gone.

"Sorry," was all he could muster.

Spupaleena nodded with a painted on smile. "We better get ready."

Pekam quickly hugged his sister and jogged off toward the horses. Her jaw dropped and her body felt dazed. Her brother had never before given her a hug. Spupaleena watched her lean, fit sibling fade into the crowd.

"Get it together," she told herself. She squared her shoulders and attempted to recite a verse Elizabeth had recently shared with her. "Trust in the Lord…um…oh, come on…" Spupaleena grabbed hold of her braids, holding her breath. Her heart beat rapidly and her face blushed. She let the air surge past her clenched teeth. "The Lord…with all your mind. No. That's not right. With all your…" She thought a moment, willing herself to breathe steadily. "With all your heart; do not…depend…on our…no, your own…"

She sighed and stomped her foot and looked up to the heavens as if asking her Creator to give her the bit of the verse she needed. *I can't think of these words in Elizabeth's tongue, how can I in my own?*

Understanding.

Spupaleena's eyes widened as she let go of her braids and searched the bushes and flowers as if the voice she heard was audible. Had Pekam spoke to her from behind a tree? No. She had watched him run off.

"Understanding, that's it." She glanced from side to side. No one. She shrugged and continued. "Seek his will in all you do," she glanced around some more, "and he will show you—me—which path I need to take." She smiled, tickled with herself for making the last part speak to her personally. She stood, wondering if the verse was from Proverbs or Psalms and would have to ask Elizabeth again. It was in one of the two, and in chapter two, no three and verse…verse…fifteen? Five? Yes, she would surely quiz her friend. Or be quizzed. Again.

Race. The Race.

Spupaleena darted off to catch up with her team and get prepared for the race. How could she have let the fool get in and bombard her thoughts and emotions? How could she have allowed such an assault to take place? She needed to put on that armor of God Elizabeth told her about. She still didn't understand it, but it sure sounded good. If she could only read and write better; too many things rolled around in that head of hers. She needed to focus.

The race. Two new teams. *Focus.*

Spupaleena glanced up and caught the scowl on Ta huht Skumhist's face. Spupaleena mouthed her sorry and checked her leggings and moccasins. She tucked in all trailing ends of buckskin ties and searched for Pekam and his team. She saw him glaring at her impatiently and acknowledged his gaze, calling over her teammates for prayer.

She rubbed Quiy Sket down, remembering why he had no saddle. Glancing around, she saw the other two of her horses and all three of Pekam's without saddles as well. She smiled and lifted her chin, proud her brother was also racing bareback. She knew he could do it having seen him practice. But he still needed confidence in himself, or so she thought. Apparently he found some courage. Somewhere. She smiled bigger. Brighter.

A crackling noise resounded from the woods several yards away. Spupaleena turned, squinting her eyes and searching the trees.

Skumhist approached his daughter. "Spupaleena, you seem rather distracted. Everything all right?" Skumhist asked.

She turned her attention to her father and slowly nodded. "Kewa, it is."

"You sure?"

She nodded. Glancing back into the woods.

"What're you looking for?"

"Loot. Nothing." She shook her head slowly, still staring into the trees.

Skumhist shifted his weight and folded his arms in front of his chest. He cleared his throat and waited. Thoughts of her coming off a horse because she failed to concentrate reeled through his mind.

Spupaleena shifted her gaze to her father, giving him a fraction of a smile.

"Are you racing today?"

Her eyes darted to the start line as she nodded. Her teammates were preparing to head out to the transition sites. Phillip held her stud, glancing at her often with a scowl crossing his face.

Spupaleena hastened to her waiting four-legged partner and hopped up onto his bare back with the grace and agility of a whitetail doe. Quiy Sket glanced back at her as if he was making sure she was alert and attentive. She rubbed his neck and quietly sang to him,

"Come and ride me, I will take you places and we will see many sites. Please baby girl, come to me…"

Hearing a cackle from her right side, she turned and noticed the tall, thin but muscular boy next to her. He looked to be nineteen or so. His hair was tightly braided and he wore a one inch, circular, abalone earring in both ears. His face had two light blue, squiggly, parallel lines that ran from the right corner of his forehead to the left side of his jaw. Spupaleena supposed it was the symbol of a creek or slender river. She had heard of these river paddlers. His tall Appaloosa, black-and-white in color, had the same two squiggly blue lines on his rump. Spupaleena eyed the boy, studying him, wanting to know if he thought her singing was amusing, or was it the fact she was a—***tuklthmeelwho*** ("Woman"). The colt pawed. The boy stared.

Clearly intimidation was his ploy. His harsh gaze fixed down at her, not speaking a word.

Spupaleena said nothing. She simply dared him with her squared shoulders and piercing gaze. Dared him to laugh at her. Dared him to suggest she be with the women on the sidelines watching with the others.

To her left came the sound of someone clearing his throat and scoffing at the same time. She shifted her eyes sideways, barely turning her head and neck. Another boy about the same age as the first examined her with half a vivid yellow sun standing out on the left side of his face, barely missing his broad nose. His buckskin shirt was tightly beaded in a brilliant yellow hue like the sun, and its bright golden rays were stamped on his black roan's rump.

The two young men exchanged glances and scarcely nodded as though they were on to some secret scheme. Spupaleena grunted and held her ground not taking her eyes off his. She refused to be intimidated by the gestures of the two swine. She had hoped the two teams would be different, accepting of a woman racer, but they appeared to be like all the others—vulgar.

At least they didn't spit at her like so many of the others had. She would give them that, but still…

The grassy valley they would be racing on was soft and could prove to be slick, but nothing as treacherous as the first race's pileup. There was no threat of snow as it was the first of May, rain perhaps, but no snow or slush. The worry at hand would be deep mud in many spots—the kind of bog that turns a horse back home. Spupaleena shivered at the thought of that wreck. She pulled herself out of the stoop and urged her horse over to where her family waited.

Focus.

Out of the blue, a verse popped into Spupaleena's mind: *This is my command—be strong and courageous! Do not be afraid or discouraged. For the Lord your God is with you where ever you go.*

Chapter 15

"Auntie Spuppy," Hannah hollered. Her screeching voice echoed through the hills.

Spupaleena turned her focus to the birdlike voice that was bouncing off rock-faced hills. She heard it again; it was her name that was being called out. *Auntie Spuppy*. Only one little person could deliver that squealing tone. She searched the crowd. Nothing. No one.

"Auntie Spuppy, over here!" Hannah waved her arm wildly as she sat on her father's shoulders. Her squirming nearly toppled him to the ground.

"She's looking for you; keep yelling. She'll find you." *Eventually*. Phillip's bum leg was tiring, but he would not give up, though he did wish he had something to plug his ears.

Spupaleena caught a glimpse of thrashing arms in the air and she smiled, waving back to the little girl.

"She saw me! She saw me!" Hannah clapped her hands and giggled in delight.

Spupaleena kept waving.

Phillip's leg was about to buckle by the time he set his overly excited daughter down.

The two Native racers, who were watching Spupaleena wave at the small girl, shook their heads, exchanged disgusted looks, and grunted in unison.

Spupaleena glanced at them both, smiled, and turned, bumping Quiy Sket with the calves of her legs, saying nothing. After a few quick steps she suddenly stopped, turned to them and said, "Hope you can stay in those pretty, little saddles of yours." She winked, turned, and trotted her stallion off. She just couldn't help herself. She knew it wasn't Christlike, but was so tired of being insulted. A little humor, she thought, never hurt.

She slid off his back, turning the reins over to a cousin and hastily went in search of a drink of water. Her mouth felt like it was as dry as the Nevada desert.

Skumhist stood a few yards off and laughed at his daughter's sense of humor, something her friends and family seldom saw. It was also a good reminder that he needed to laugh more. He turned to go and gather the two teams of his children and whoever else would help pray over them.

Quiy Sket whinnied as he saw his owner approaching him. He was now settled into his routine and he was ready—calm, strong, and focused. Spupaleena stopped in front of him and reached up to stroke his soft nose. She quickly tightened the three strands of buckskin, fastening three adult eagle feathers to his mane. Her cousin smiled and handed the reins back to her. Spupaleena thanked the girl and scanned the outskirts of the crowd until she located her father.

It was time to pray.

"Spupaleena!" Ta huht Skumhist hollered. The crowd was so thick the girl had to elbow her way through.

"Over here." Spupaleena waved both hands in the air. Quiy Sket jerked his ears forward, watching his owner with curiosity.

Ta huht Skumhist struggled to make her way to her friend's side.

"Ready?" Spupaleena asked.

"Kewa. Where is everyone?"

"Over by that big fir tree." Spupaleena pointed in the direction they needed to go, standing on her tiptoes.

Ta huht Skumhist bobbed her head in agreement.

Once they had arrived, the teammates gathered up the horses and painted on the three purple crosses lining the stallions' necks and checked to make sure each one had tightened the three eagle feathers on their manes. Pekam's team soon joined them and they all stood in a circle with family members laying hands on the two riders, eight handlers, and six horses.

Skumhist led them in prayer asking the Creator God for safety, wisdom, and for each member to honor the Lord and his Son, shedding off any selfish motivation. That each team member would act in a way that would bring tribute to God. When he had finished, racers took off for their respective sites and family members scattered in search of their favorite spots to watch and cheer on both teams. Skumhist stayed behind to walk with both of his children to the staging area.

Spupaleena glanced in the direction of where she saw Phillip and Hannah. Skumhist smiled knowing who she was searching for.

"She's still here, don't worry, stumpkeelt."

Spupaleena stared ahead, smiling. She took her father's hand in hers and squeezed it tightly.

"They'll leave after the race." He returned the gesture.

Spupaleena nodded. As long as she knew Elizabeth was watching and praying today, that was all she needed to know. There was a great deal at stake with this race because many potential friends from the Kettle Falls, whom they traded with, were to show up and consider Quiy Sket for breeding. Word from a cousin promised half a dozen prospects. This was the break she had been praying for—someone finally taking her seriously as a trainer, racer, and finally a breeder.

Her chest pounded as they walked. Thoughts of deals being made reeled through her mind and she squeezed her father's hand tightly. But for now, she needed to concentrate on those liquid smooth transitions. She played those exchanges over and over in her mind until she finally made her way to the starting area.

Skumhist turned and hugged his daughter. He gazed into her eyes for several seconds, leaving a message of assurance stamped in her heart. He then turned to Pekam, placed a hand on either side of his head, pulling his son's forehead to his own, praying for protection. Skumhist willed himself to remain strong and confident so his son would emulate the same.

"Be safe, squasee," Skumhist whispered. He attempted to hide his distress.

Pekam nodded, giving his father a self-assured look. He saw the worry in his father's eyes and it sent chills coursing throughout his body. The boy swallowed hard, struggling to keep his courage intact.

Skumhist turned to go and find the Gardners.

Spupaleena hopped up on Quiy S<u>k</u>et, sitting tall, with her legs dangling at the stallion's sides. She wanted to flow with him, not sit too relaxed and certainly not too stiff. While taking a few minutes to bend and soften the red roan, his ears began to flicker in the direction of the crowd cheering for the favored riders. Once she took hold of the reins, asking for him to collect and bend in each direction at a smooth trot, his ears focused back on her. She could feel him relax into a soft, even rhythm.

Hearing the birdlike whistle, she reined him to a halt and took a few seconds to rub his neck. She then gave him his head and let him walk to the start line. Keeping Quiy S<u>k</u>et quiet proved to be an advantage for him. He was quicker off the start line and was able to surge with power while the other horses were still scrambling to get their bearings straight. While they waited, she sang to him, "Baby girl, baby girl, tell me what do you see, an orange pony, a yellow pony, a purple pony. Kewa, three."

Spupaleena could feel sordid eyes pitched on her. She just kept singing in a low, soothing voice. Pekam was to his sister's right and she thought she could hear him talking to See<u>ch</u> Sneewt, trying to calm the brown-and-white Overo. A smile grew on her face. She was still shocked that Elizabeth gave the horse to Pekam. Her brother was more taken back as to the reason why—in memory of her deceased first born son. Her heart was bigger than any Spupaleena had ever known.

Elizabeth had told Pekam to ride for the tiny, two-pound baby boy and that someday they would meet in heaven. The boy choked back tears as he nodded. He would also be united with his brother who passed as a toddler, **K̲ook̲yuma May Ooya** ("Little Raccoon"), and what a day that would be.

Focus.

The whooping and hollering echoed off the hills as the horses danced and pawed knowing the start cry would come momentarily. The K̲alispeliwho rider struggled to keep his stout Appaloosa stallion focused and quiet as did the Spukanee rider and his leggy roan. Brisk electricity ran through the damp air sparking the energy of everyone present. Riders could barely hold back their horses and for some reason, that start cry seemed to take forever. Even the still Quiy Sk̲et was beginning to squirm.

Spupaleena caught sight of Ska ka ka. He wore the symbol of a white salmon across his nose that stretched from cheek to cheek, a symbol of peace and strength. They eyed one another respectfully and nodded in good will. Pelpalwheechula was no doubt on one of the exchanges; she was more than likely at the last leg as she was strong and her timing was perfect. The girl would send Ska ka ka off on one powerful push for the home stretch.

Finally it came. A Native man perched high in a tree sounded the call. Horses sped off and dirt flew.

The crowd cheered, not caring if the muddy clods struck them or not.

Spupaleena grabbed a hold of Quiy S<u>k</u>et's mane and they instantly took the lead.

Pekam and See<u>ch</u> Sneewt blew off the line. The stallion burst so quickly his rider nearly toppled off.

The Spukanee and <u>K</u>alispeli<u>who</u> riders were on his tail.

The rest lagged behind a half length or more.

Quiy S<u>k</u>et took to being ridden bareback as though he'd done it for years. He nosed ahead and ate up the ground like he was being chased by a pack of wolves. Spupaleena could feel his bulging muscles as each hoof hit the ground and was lifted back into the air. Smooth. Rhythmical. They flew down the lane and it felt good.

Quiy S<u>k</u>et's right ear flicked back and she knew someone was quickly approaching. Glancing over her shoulder, she saw her little brother's determined look spread over his face. He loved his sister, but this was a race and he had every right to ride hard and win. He was not holding back and neither were the others as a flash of yellow and blue were hot on their heels.

Spupaleena reached her arms forward and just let the stallion run. Quiy S<u>k</u>et didn't need a reminder from her whip, only from her passion. He could feel her heart beating and he charged forward. She let that passion flow, passion for riding, passion for Quiy S<u>k</u>et, and passion for the God who put the dream in her heart. *Trust in Him at all times...pour out your heart, for God is our refuge.*

As the handlers and horses for the next exchange came into view, Quiy Sket veered for Kookyuma In-tee-tee-huh. He pinned his ears and eyes on that purple figure wildly jumping about, shouting his name. He knew the voice and the color of the one who would safely catch him and give him rest. Spupaleena readied herself to hop off one mount and lunge onto the next. She drew in a breath as she watched Kookyuma In-tee-tee-huh call them in.

Spupaleena let out that breath through relaxed lips, gently tugged back on the reins, and sank into her horse's back, asking him to slow down. He took her cue and began to reduce his speed as his hind quarters collected underneath himself and his front legs acted as brakes. His body curved into the other horses and they too slowed down, keeping from crashing into each other. Spupaleena fluidly slid off the red roan, took three steps, and lifted herself on the back of the squirrely sorrel-and-white Overo.

Noonwheena took off like a flash of lightening. Spupaleena grabbed a hunk of mane and held on. She leaned forward and gave the spry horse a few taps on the rump with the whip Phillip had crafted for her. His front legs stretched and the animal sped up, keeping them in the lead. His left ear flicked back and forth. Spupaleena kept her focus on the rock bluff ahead not looking back at the approaching horse. She hoped it was still her brother.

Cold air slapped her face like a wet rag, and her eyes watered and stung. She blinked the pain away and squinted into the sun. She lowered her chin to cut the wind, softly urging the big horse on. Out of the corner of her eye, she saw the roan catching her and trying to pass. Noonwheena thrust ahead as the pair traded off as the forerunner.

Around the bend was a soft patch of fresh grass. The riders knew it would be touch and go as they would sling around the corner. Spupaleena relaxed her body as best she could and tightened the hold on the chunk of mane in her hand. She wanted her balance to help Noonwheena, not hinder him. She forced herself to breathe slowly and steadily—in and out, in and out. She prayed for both solid footing and courage for her mount.

She heard a yell from behind as a black horse slipped and fell. The Spukanee rider was tossed to the ground, skidding to a stop. He caught his horse, jumped back on, and tore off. Pekam galloped past him while the jilted rider was sliding across the wet grass. The Kalispeliwho rider was further behind; he had tripped on the last exchange and rolled beneath the waiting horse. He quickly scrambled to his feet, climbed up into the saddle, and was nearly caught up to Ska ka ka, Inchechun, and Cheelkst Kawup, who were all in a tight pack when they rounded the corner.

The third and last exchange was just ahead. The riders would have to cross a small creek first, make the transfer, and rush down a narrow hill. They would all have to jump a thin gulley before reaching the finish line.

Spupaleena was coming up on the creek when she noticed the fool crouching near a thick pine. He was watching her and that made an evil feeling run up and down her spine. But something was different and it caught her off guard. She had no time to ponder him and turned her thoughts back to the race. She pinned her gaze on the creek and in no time Noonwheena crossed it with little effort. *He was here, watching her. The look on his face was...*

Spupaleena's thoughts were interrupted by Chy chy pum Sn'e who was shouting her name. She was coming in too fast, not paying attention. Her horse was leaning toward the voice calling his name, but she was busy with her thoughts shifting back and forth from the fool to the race. She grabbed hold of the rein and pulled back as Noonwheena fought the bit. He slowed down, but not before careening into Chy chy pum Sn'e, knocking him to the ground.

Spupaleena shouted his name and jumped off the horse, lost her footing, and rolled on the damp grass. She instinctively went to help him up, but he yelled for her to go, pointing to Spaoos Newt. She jumped to her feet as Hun Han neekun, who scowled at the lack of concentration her teammate exhibited, scooted the massive bay over so Spupaleena could get her strides and lunge up on his back.

Once on, Spupaleena kicked and shouted to get the stallion running. She was now behind her brother, knowing he had snuck in the lead as she was rolling around in the grass. She gritted her teeth and slapped the whip across her horse's rump. She prayed for a pinch of safety and a bucketful of speed.

Seelwha Sn'e was about to catch Pekam's horse. Her brother's best skill was the transfers; he was light and smooth on his feet. His arms were scrawny but strong, stronger than his sisters. But she had experience on her side and packed a few pounds less than he did. The catch could not have been more perfect and Pekam effortlessly glided onto the back of the waiting mount and sped off.

Pekam had been awe struck as he rode past his sister. He chuckled at the sight of her rolling around on the ground, knowing she would be fuming by the time she crawled on her horse. His smile was so huge his face hurt. Could he really beat his big sister? It was too good to be true.

Caught off guard, Pekam's stomach felt like it was in his throat as he and his horse dashed down a hill. He was now out of sorts due to his own prideful and distracting thoughts that silently laughed at his sister. He saw his horse's ear swivel to the side and knew she was close. It had to be her. No one else could have caught up that fast, and Pekam knew his sister was quick on her feet and red-hot mad. He snickered and forced himself to be serious and turn his wayward thoughts to finishing this race and for once win—against his sister.

Spupaleena soon forgot about the fool and had her little brother in her sites. She was catching up to Ska ka ka with the Spukanee rider close behind. Their transfers weren't as smooth as hers costing them valuable time, but not much. The others were a few horse lengths away and bringing up the rear. All Spupaleena could think about was catching her brother, passing him, and taking the win for herself. She was not ready to let him snatch that away from her.

Chapter 16

Hahoola<u>who</u> knelt down beside the pine tree and wept as he watched the girl race by on the horse he once owned. He was sorry. Sorry for his pride. Sorry for his bitterness. Sorry he was so set on vengeance, actually attempting to poison someone else's animals. Who had he become? What turned his heart so cold and evil? Shame filled every fiber in his body and he trembled, watching Spupaleena sprint past him on the horse he lost to her. A tear slid down his cheek and he wiped it away with the back of his hand. He recently considered her the enemy. How could he? She never tried to harm him, or anyone. She merely wished to race her horses.

Regret consumed him in a way that his chest tightened and made him gasp for air. Kneeling in the wet grass, he prayed and asked the Creator to forgive him and give him a new heart—a second chance. One filled with love and the courage to overcome his wrong ways and start living a life that would bring respect, trust, and honor to his family. He had only shamed them, especially his mother who deserved better.

Quiy Ha-hau's illness had made Hahoola<u>who</u> rethink the bitterness that was eating at his soul. He was tired of people in his life leaving. Having thought his father was on his way out and for the first time that he could remember, Hahoola<u>who</u> cared for someone other than himself. Sickness had slapped him in the face with the force of a stallion's back hooves against his chest. The sorrow in his mother's eyes made his heart sink; he didn't want his father to leave them. He shuddered at the image of his mother's tears as she wiped a cool cloth over her husband's forehead. He knew his father's harshness was only trying to make him grow up strong. He hated the man's sharp tongue, but he loved his father nonetheless.

Someday Hahoola<u>who</u> would talk with Spupaleena and ask her forgiveness. He was tired of being angry. He was tired of hating. Spupaleena deserved better and in the meantime, he would have to pray for the nerve to approach her with a renewed heart. More than likely, she would not receive him with open arms, but a clenched fist. A well earned one at that.

When Quiy Ha-hau had finally woke up, he called for his son to come and sit with him. The ill man shared how the Creator had come to him in a dream, telling him how wrong his harshness had been toward his son. He asked Hahoola<u>who</u> for forgiveness; tears streaming down his face. He also asked his wife for the same merciful pardon while in the presence of their son, and Hahoola<u>who</u> was amazed at the grace his mother bestowed on her husband. It was then the fool knew what he had to do.

He hurried to his horse and rushed to the race. He had to see it; he had to know how it all turned out. He wanted the girl to succeed. She had every right to train and ride—to win. He didn't yet have the courage to approach her, but some day…

Hahoola<u>who</u> was so filled with emotion, he felt the need to kneel and pray. He pled for safety over Spupaleena and the other racers. As he finished, a surge of quiet peace settled over him as though the Creator was wrapping his arms around the young man. He stood and quickly made his way to the finish line, staying out of sight, at least for now. He figured no one really wanted to see him and for good reason. It would be a long and windy road to the day he could be trusted, possibly for the first time. Another first was what he was feeling at that moment—serenity.

He climbed to the top of a rock cliff and perched on a good sized rock behind scrub brush and young fir trees, watching the rest of the race. He secretly hoped the girl would win but was not ready to say it aloud. His heart had changed, but letting go of some old habits and attitudes would remain a struggle. Change would come slowly but surely.

Spaoos Newt tore down the hill spraying wet sand in all directions. Spupaleena could feel his heart pound on her legs. His hooves left deep pits in the earth and his chest heaved with each gasp of air he took in. Spupaleena slid all over his sweat-coated back like a chipmunk trying to climb up a wet mossy boulder. Her legs and fingers ached from exhaustion, but she clung tight. Her fingernails dug into her palms leaving indentations as she hung onto rein and mane.

Spupaleena felt the power of her stallion's hindquarters kick in as he reached forward with every ounce of gumption he had left. He seemed to want to win as badly as she did. With one more challenging obstacle to go, Spupaleena could feel the power of his strength and will kick in as he ran. She could see it in his eyes when they rounded a corner. They rode as one, not separate entities, and were quickly approaching Pekam.

Pekam's horse's left ear flicked back and forth as the animal surged ahead. He leaned forward with his eyes frontward and with his arms reaching up the horse's neck. He gave the bit to his stallion and let him fly. Pekam saw the finish rope several yards ahead; he still refused to glance back. He pinned his focus on that end mark and stuck to the horse as though a good helping of pitch kept him there.

The three-foot gully was quickly approaching and in mere seconds it would be right in front of their faces. Spupaleena was now at her brother's side and a wide grin spread on her face. Hooves were pounding the wet earth, sides were heaving, and sweat was sliding down the legs of the unwavering animals. Neither horse nor rider was about to give up.

In unison, Spupaleena and Pekam's horses left the ground and soared over the gully, hitting the ground at the same time—a picture perfect moment—one Spupaleena wished she could freeze forever. The instant Spaoos Newt's hooves touched the dirt, he summoned any remaining energy and pitched ahead, crossing the finish rope a hair before Pekam's breathless stallion.

The other riders and their exhausted mounts were pushing hard for the finish line and not far behind. The third rider to come in was the Spukanee rider, then Ska ka ka, the K̲alispeliw̲ho, Inche̲chun, and finally C̲heelkst Kawup, who never really was able to get his horse up to speed.

Spupaleena reined Spaoos Newt to a halt as the others flew passed. Pekam still had to work on his red roan's stop. On the last leg he had the better push of speed, but getting the fifteen-year-old stud to slow down and halt when the adrenalin coursed through his body was no easy task, especially for a young teenage boy. Pekam was able to get a hold of Seec̲h Sneewt's head and circle the big roan around until his feet stopped. He rubbed the horse's neck, proud of his run. It didn't matter if his sister won, he was proud of her. Besides, there would be other times and more races. To come in second against the greatest racer around the territory, in his eyes, was nothing short of a miracle.

As the riders approached the starting area, the crowd burst out into cheers for Spupaleena as word had quickly spread of her feat.

The K̲alispeliw̲ho rider and Spukanee rider walked up to Spupaleena stone faced. Her heart raced and her body stiffened, ready to block hurling insults. To her surprise they both broke out into teeth baring smiles.

"I was wrong about you," the Spukanee rider said in his Native tongue, which was close enough to her own that Spupaleena understood the meaning.

"Me, too. You're a swift and strong rider and I would like to learn more from you. You handle your horse differently and I want to learn those ways," the Kalispeliwho rider said in his own language. Again she knew enough to understand his meaning.

Spupaleena stood with her mouth gaping, wondering if what she was hearing was really true.

The Spukanee rider nodded in agreement as he glanced from the Kalispeliwho to Spupaleena.

She peered at both of their faces, watching the sweat streak their paint. No one had ever asked for advice, let alone to train with her. Excitement bubbled in her chest, yet she was reluctant to show it. How will they train? Who will all come? Where? Questions flooded her mind. She needed a plan.

Spupaleena slowly nodded as a thought drifted into her mind. "We will leave in five days"—she held up five fingers—"to my friend's house near your summer camp." She pointed to the Spukanee rider.

The young men exchanged glances and nodded. They agreed to meet later and make their plans. Spupaleena hoped this wasn't a trap set by the enemy to tip her off balance. She would bring the matter up with her father later and pray. She could always call it off.

As she walked to stake her horse out, the image of Hahoolawho came to her mind. The angry snakelike features and beady eyes were replaced with an expression filled with sorrow and remorse. She heard news of his father's recovery. Maybe that had something to do with it. She shook her head and asked God to bless him. Suddenly, she stopped. *Pray for him?* Until now, that was the last thing on her mind.

Pray for him. The Holy Spirit filled her with comfort as she hid her face in her hands and wept, asking God to forgive her. She should have been praying for him and his team the whole time. Not fighting him, but praying as Elizabeth had read to her from the Bible. She felt shame as the word *fool* spun through her thoughts. Yes, he had acted like a fool, but that was a battle for Jesus, not her. She should have loved and prayed, not criticized.

Skumhist saw the distress on his daughter's face and walked up to her, gathering her in his arms. He held her tight while she sobbed on his shoulder. "I don't know what troubles you stumpkeelt, but you *will* get through it."

She clung to her father and let him soothe her shattered heart. She had won today's race, yet would celebrate a greater reward later with her family—the gift of forgiveness. She stood in the middle of the bustling crowd, clutching her father, praying silently as she thanked God for his never ending grace.

Chapter 17

Hannah squealed with delight. "She's really mine?"

Both Phillip and Elizabeth smiled brightly as they watched their daughter lavish the pint-sized sorrel-and-white mare with hugs and kisses.

"Yes, she's really yours." Elizabeth brushed a tendril of loose hair from her face and pinned it back in her bun. "Thank your papa. He traded a cow for her."

Hannah thrust the lead rope in her mother's hands and ran for her father. He bent down and picked her up and they twirled around, laughing. Phillip tickled her, making her giggle even harder. Delbert joined in the celebration by grabbing hold of his father's leg and jumping up and down hollering—"*horthy*"—over and over again.

Phillip leaned over and scooped up his son, twirling them both in the air, yelling and giggling. Lillian clapped her hands, squealing and kicking her legs as she watched them from the protection of her mother's arms.

"What's this all about?" Spupaleena said as she ambled up to the boisterous family.

Phillip stopped and let Hannah down. She ran to her auntie and grabbed her hand, leading Spupaleena over to her new pony. "She's mine, all mine. I love her. Isn't she pretty?" Hannah hugged her pony tightly. The pony tripped sideways, but the girl hung on tight. She wasn't about to let go of the best gift she had ever received. After some time, she did release her grip, stroking her tiny hand on the pony's miniature nose.

"Kewa, she's a nice one." Spupaleena looked at the Gardners, her brows arched and the corners of her mouth turned up as a glint formed in her eyes.

"I know. We gave in." Phillip put Delbert down and held up his hands. "What can I say? I have a soft spot for making my kids happy."

"How did this happen?" Spupaleena turned to Elizabeth. She rubbed her hands together, stifling a chuckle.

"Well, we thought about what you said. She has such a desire to race, we thought it would be better to teach her now; hoping later that desire may just dissipate right out of her thoughts. If not, she would at least have the proper training." Elizabeth paused. The corners of her mouth turned up and a twinkle in her eye appeared. "The funniest part was when Phillip bartered for her."

"He what?" Spupaleena laughed. "What could you possibly give my people that they already don't have?" She smiled teasingly.

"A cow." Phillip raked his fingers through his hair.

Spupaleena burst out laughing. "What will they do with a cow?" She clapped her hands together.

He snorted. "She'll come with a calf and be useful for milk."

"Are you teasing?"

Phillip laughed. "No. I'm quite serious." He barely choked out his words as the red in his face deepened.

"A milk cow? Someone actually traded a pony for a milk cow? I guess you got the good end of the deal." Spupaleena shook her head. Her people were unaccustomed to milk, and she hoped they would like the taste. They would surely need to learn how to process it like she had seen Elizabeth do. "I wonder what Jack will say?" Elizabeth chuckled. "Are you kidding? You know Jack and horses. He'll know *they* got the best end of this deal."

Spupaleena beamed. "You're probably right. I can't wait to see his face."

Elizabeth turned to watch her daughter who was attempting to place her little foot in the tiny stirrup with no success. She smiled and knew they had made a good trade.

"What're you going to name your pony, Hannah?" Spupaleena asked.

The girl stopped with her foot in midair, plopped it back on the ground, and thought a moment. Finally she blurted out, "Angel Spirit." She nodded her head, proud of the name she had come up with.

Spupaleena smiled. She was impressed with the young girl's choice.

Elizabeth nodded and asked, "How'd you come up with her name?"

"Because she's like an angel's spirit—she protects me." Hannah giggled and went back to her best attempts at reaching her booted foot into the stirrup.

Phillip beamed with pride. He had always felt the names he and Jack gave their horses had meaning. "She gets that from me." He said, grinning.

Spupaleena and Elizabeth exchanged wide-eyed glances and burst out laughing. Lillian squealed and Phillip reached for her. He had to have someone on his side. Elizabeth passed off the little one and went for Delbert, who was trying to dangle off Angel Spirit's tail.

"On a serious note, it's time for us to pack up and go home." Phillip said.

"I know. I'm coming, too."

"You are?" Elizabeth and Hannah said in unison. Hannah dropped the lead rope and headed for another of her auntie's warm hugs. Spupaleena's stern look stopped the girl in her tracks and she turned, picking up the lead then placing it in her mother's waiting hand, and ran for those outstretched arms. Elizabeth shook her head as an easy grin spread over her features. *What a pair*, she thought.

"Kewa, all of us are coming." Spupaleena gestured toward her and Pekam's teams who were busily packing. I need to go and help, but just stopped to see what the commotion was all about."

Phillip nodded. "When are you leaving?"

"In the morning. We still have a lot of packing to do." Spupaleena grabbed her braids. "We'll meet up with the Spukanee and Kalispel<u>who</u> teams on the other side of the Columbia River."

"Good, we'll wait and travel with you then instead of leaving today." Phillip shifted his weight off his bum leg and looked at Spupaleena. "Besides, I need to update my roster." He turned and winked at his wife.

"Kewa, I like that idea. We can all help. I like your roster. It has helped me concentrate on what I need to do to beat my opponents." Spupaleena glanced at Elizabeth who winked at her, eyes gleaming. Spupaleena paused in order to keep serious, and then tipped her head in her father's direction. "He decided to tag along."

"How'd you manage that?" Elizabeth asked.

Spupaleena shrugged her shoulders. "He asked."

Phillip and his wife exchanged pleased glances.

"I can't wait to show him more of the local herbs I've discovered."

"I'm sure my mistum's counting on that."

Spupaleena gave Hannah one last squeeze and then turned to leave.

"You said the two other teams were joining us?" Elizabeth raised a brow.

Spupaleena chuckled. "They want to learn some training and riding methods from me." She swallowed. "Never thought that would ever happen."

"Why? You're good with horses and a talented rider; it was bound to happen sooner or later," Phillip said, his words made her blush.

Spupaleena stammered. "I guess." She stood a moment not knowing what to do or say, then quickly turned and headed for the others.

Morning came early and the pack of humans and horses walked out of the village just as the first light announced the start of the day. Spring would soon turn the corner and let summer take root. Spupaleena looked forward to those warm summer nights, where the crickets sang and the coyotes yelped.

Spupaleena smiled as they headed for the river and the sandy crossing where her colt, Nee Ap Kukneeya, had gotten away from her last summer. She did miss him, but was thankful he ended up in a good home. She drew in a deep breath permitting the fresh air to expand her lungs, hoping it would awaken her mind and quicken her reflexes.

By now the water was receding and crossing it would be somewhat safer, but they still needed to be cautious.

Hannah sat cradled in her father's lap, dazed in the glow of morning. He led her pony while Elizabeth carried Lillian on her back. She had already fallen back to sleep. Skumhist offered to let Delbert ride with him, and the toddler was fast asleep in his arms.

The crossing would be tricky, but they were used to it. Spupaleena decided to stay close to Elizabeth and the baby while Pekam watched Phillip, Hannah, and the pony; he was ready to assist if the time came. The current still ran strong from the snow pack, but not nearly as bad as when Phillip and Elizabeth crossed it earlier. They took special precautions due to the little ones. They stopped at the water line and Skumhist glanced at everyone, nodded, and let his horse step into the water.

Pekam and Phillip followed with the ladies close behind. They were flanked by the rest of the teammates, who were closely watching Elizabeth and the sleeping baby strapped on her back. She was tucked in tightly with the special buckskin backpack Phillip designed for the longer rides. The infant was warm and comfortable with her head and neck secured by a thin, rolled-up baby quilt in case they needed to gallop. One never knew when they would encounter a mountain lion; it was best to be prepared.

The horses picked their way across the rocky bottom toward the middle of the river. Some parts were knee deep, and others were belly deep or more. The frigid water was breath taking as it flowed into their boots and moccasins, and the riders sucked in a quick breath as they felt it on their calves and feet. Knowing the iced pain wouldn't last long, not one complaint escaped their lips.

It didn't take long for everyone to cross the creek and hop up to the trail leading south. Soon they would meet up with their new friends and head to the Gardners.

Chapter 18

Jack stood tall. He wore his usual black Stetson and colored neckerchief tied neatly around his neck. "The boys can stay with me." He eyed the team members from the Spukanee and Kalispeli<u>who</u> people in a protective manner, that of a father to his daughter.

A chuckle slipped out of Spupaleena's mouth, "Kewa. That would be fine. I'll stay with Elizabeth and get in a few more writing lessons at night. We didn't have enough time to finish the last arithmetic lesson. Nor the spelling lesson for that matter. Can't seem to get words like pair and pare straight."

Jack looked at her and scowled. "We don't know these boys that well. I'm not taking any chances."

"I know. I agree, *mistum*." She did have to admit that his shielding ways made her feel safe. Massive Jack against the scrawny Native boys; she watched him searching them for the slightest hint of wrong doing.

Jack shook his head, his spine rigid and his legs set wide as if to scare away any inappropriate thoughts those young men might be having.

"How's things going?" Phillip asked as he hobbled up to the pair.

"Fine." Jack said stiffly.

Spupaleena rolled her eyes to the heavens. "Kewa, good. Mistum here is getting his feathers ruffled."

"Oh? How's that?" Phillip leaned against the corral Dusty stood in. He snorted and shook his head, ready to start training while Quiy S<u>k</u>et would be back to breeding once again.

"Do you trust these whelps?" Jack tore off his Stetson and slammed it against his knee, knocking off the dust.

"Jack, they said nothing but nice things to me at the race. They're to be trusted. My mistum, the real one, talked to them thoroughly and passed his grueling test of…of…"

"Character?" Elizabeth offered as she walked up to the group with a content infant in her arms.

"Kewa, character." Spupaleena turned to face her friend, feeling her heartbeat speed up. "They'll be just fine, Jack. Really."

"Yeah? What do you think, Phillip?" Jack placed his Stetson back on his head.

"Come on, they're nice and only want to learn our ways of training. They recognize that our methods work better than the ones they've been taught. They just want to ride."

"Well?" Jack persisted.

Phillip sighed. "I think they'll behave. I was there when Skumhist drilled them, and they were very respectful. Almost thanking him for setting such ridged boundaries."

Jack nodded. "All right then. But they're staying with me and that's final."

"Good." The rest said in unison. They glanced at one another and snickered. Even Jack loosened up a bit and smiled—with one eye watching those boys, of course.

"Pekam and his team can stay here with me." Spupaleena announced.

"There's plenty of room by the garden, as long as they don't try to snack on my wife's hard work," Phillip teased.

Spupaleena reached for Lillian and cradled the baby in her arms. "You better watch out my little angel, Uncle Jack will be guarding you just as tightly someday." Lillian cooed and smiled as though she was agreeing with her auntie.

Phillip and Elizabeth laughed.

Jack just grunted and walked off.

Spupaleena chuckled and watched the gentle giant as he strode over with his extra long legs to the waiting bunch of hungry young men.

The next morning, everyone was up early. Spupaleena was eager to jump on Dusty, bareback she figured, and begin practicing their transitions. If she exchanged fluidly with no saddle, it would be a cinch with one on.

"Wi, lthkickha. Ready for today? For me to beat you this time?" Pekam spoke with a glint in his eye.

Spupaleena reached over and grabbed hold of his shirt sleeve. She smiled widely. "You? Beat me? Never sintahoos. My horse is faster, stronger, and much wiser than your sinewy kid's pony." She laughed heartily.

Pekam jerked his arm away and lifted her in the air. He pinned her arms to her sides as he whirled her around, trying to make her dizzy. Spupaleena squealed and wiggled, but couldn't break loose. She laughed and kicked until Pekam finally set her down as if she were a porcelain doll. She staggered a few strides as her brother laughed and tickled her sides.

"I will"—Spupaleena laughed so hard she could barely muster the words—"leave your old nag and you in the dirt…you will eat our dust."

"Oh, we will, will we?" Pekam tugged her braids and jogged off, his cackles echoing off the hill sides.

Spupaleena smiled. She made her way to the corral where Dusty was lazing in the warmth of the morning sun and loosened her muscles with a few stretches. Dusty craned his neck in her direction as if it was loaded down with a sack of rocks. He groaned, asking for more time in the sun's rays.

"Come on big man, you've had plenty of time resting. Let's get you ready, boy." Spupaleena stretched to the sky as high as her hands could reach and she wiggled her fingers as a bird flew overhead. She smiled with her face to the sun. She tingled all over as she thought of reuniting with her stallion.

"Are you not ready yet?" Ta <u>huht</u> Skumhist growled as she sat impatiently on the Overo's back. Spaoos Newt's eyes were alert, glancing around while his ears swiveled about.

"Almost. Don't you just love these warm mornings? Look at those hills"—she nodded in their direction—"covered in those purple spring flowers. What are those called, do you know?" Spupaleena shaded her eyes with her hands. Ta <u>huh</u>t Skumhist groaned, shaking her head. "You're asking me? I don't know what's getting into you lately with your bright, smelly flowers. We have horses to work and races to run. Get in the game, will you?" She plunked her hands on her hips, and her feet were wiggling in the air as if they alone could spark some motion into Spupaleena's laidback demeanor.

"I'm ready." Spupaleena giggled. "Just discovering that there's more to this world than racing, even though racing definitely is important…" Her voice trailed off as she spoke. She took in a deep breath through her nose, smelling the sweet scents wafting through the air. "You cause grass to grow for the livestock and plants for people to use. You allow them to produce food from the earth and herbs for medicine. Thank you, Lord, for all you give to us. Let me never again take it for granted." Spupaleena closed her eyes for a moment and soaked in the Lord's presence as he spoke to her heart.

Ta <u>huh</u>t Skumhist rolled her eyes. "I'll meet you over there." She jerked her skinny finger in the direction of the others who were waiting in the shade of the fir trees that lead the way toward Jack's place. She shared the same God, but just didn't feel the need to pray over every little bit of creation.

"Be right there." Spupaleena smiled at her fidgety friend. She opened the gate and strode to Dusty.

Rubbing his soft neck, she talked to him in a hushed voice then slipped the grass stained bit into his mouth and led him out the gate.

She took her trademark run-skip-hop and was on Dusty's back as quick as the blink of an eye. Phillip nodded and they rode off. It didn't take long to catch up to the others.

For the next several days, Jack, Spupaleena, and Pekam taught the visitors how to soften their horses and work toward a nice solid stop. They rode in the hills, around the bushes, and through the cows. Their new friends constantly exchanged quizzical glances with one another, especially the first couple of days, but quickly saw how the gentle methods caused their horses to be more responsive and less reactive.

"That's better," Jack would periodically say as he swelled with pride. He felt like a mother hen with her chicks, or what he assumed that would feel like. He had expected a tougher time teaching these no-good accounts, but quickly learned how wrong he had been about them. He was finally able to admit to himself that he had been sorely wrong about these boys. He even asked God to forgive his sour attitude—after the Holy Spirit convicted him that his snarly mindset was nothing but sinful pride and not the protective manner he tried to pass it off to be.

Jack watched Spupaleena canter Dusty and something just wasn't right. "How does he feel?" His brow furrowed and the corners of his mouth turned down.

"Loot, not so good. He's not as strong. I don't understand. He was fine for you. I...I just don't know what's wrong?"

"Jump off and let's check for heat."

Spupaleena circled and pulled him to a halt. She hopped off and Jack felt for heat on one side and Spupaleena ran her hands down his legs on the other. Each hoof was picked up and checked for stone bruises. On his right hoof there looked to be a reddish splotch. Spupaleena called Jack over to examine it.

"He's going to need some rest. Take a few days off and soak his hoof in the creek. There's not much we can do." Jack rubbed his chin with his gloved fingers.

"Do you think he'll be ready for this next race?"

"When is it?"

"We have two weeks."

Spupaleena stood and rubbed Dusty's neck. Jack stood and stretched his stiff back muscles. "Maybe. I guess we'll have to wait and see."

"I can always bring Quiy Sket back with me. He did great the last race."

Jack nodded as different scenarios raced through his head. He grunted and walked back to his horse.

Because the Kalispeli<u>who</u>s and Spukanees were already accomplished riders, they progressed rapidly. The horses started enjoying their jobs and the riders actually wore smiles on their faces. Every so often, a little ribbing would take place and bets would be made of who would win the next practice race. By the end of the week, the Spukanee and Kalispeli<u>who</u> teammates were all making their transfers gracefully. Soon they'd head south to race with teams in the Oregon Territory. She knew they would be ready and willing to keep up with their workouts. Jack spoke with them, sharing ways to continue advancing their training. He showed them how to bend their horses' rib cages and do maneuvers to get all parts of their body soft and willing.

Their eyes lit up with the increased knowledge and confidence.

That night they all gathered at the Gardner's place. Everyone was laughing and reminiscing over fun times of training and learning they all shared the past few days. Chores were finished and the guest teams were settled around the fire. The Spukanees and Kalispeli<u>who</u>s motioned their hosts over to sit with them. Once everyone was settled, the men began to pass out gifts to Spupaleena, Pekam, Jack, and Phillip for their appreciation.

"Lim lumt," Spupaleena said. She stared down at the beautiful wool coat they gifted her with and the matching beaded necklace. Their brilliant hues of yellow, green, orange, and red striping radiated in the glow of their evening fire. She held on to them with thanksgiving.

"Here for you." The Kalispeli<u>who</u> held out a freshly carved bow and quiver thick with arrows. Pekam froze. He looked at his sister, who nodded. He reached his trembling hands out and let the man place the gift in his open palms.

"Lim lumt," was all he could muster. His eyes were wide with unbelief.

Next another teammate held out a traditional spear to Phillip while another man offered a beaded buckskin jacket to Jack. His guard by then had collapsed only leaving a sense of family with the young men. He realized these boys truly had character, more than most he had seen at their young age.

Phillip and Jack peered at one another, holding their gaze for a few seconds. They smiled brightly in the light of the crackling fire and reached for their gifts. None of which were expected. Jack choked out his, "Thank you" and Phillip stood and shook their hands.

Each female team member received a beaded necklace and each male team member, as well as Skumhist, were handed a brightly colored wool blanket. Elizabeth was given a beaded necklace and bracelet and the children also received little handcrafted toys from their guests' tribes.

"You have given us more than we could ever expect. Please accept these gifts. Tonight we dance and sing and share each other's company. Tomorrow we will head south for the Oregon lands," the Spukanee leader said. The group did just that while drinking some of Elizabeth's sweetened tea and snacking on dried fish and jerked beef.

The following morning, Elizabeth and Skumhist took the time to point out additional local herbs to the Kalispeli<u>who</u> and Spukanee racers for cuts, bruises, colic, and soreness. They picked a nice assortment for their travels. Skumhist gathered various herbs for Dusty's bruised hoof, as well, and Elizabeth sewed little pouches from scrap leather for each herb and drew the flower on each bag for easy identification. It was the least they could do.

Chapter 19

It was the last day. Phillip and the others would be back late as they were all celebrating the success of the Kalispeli<u>who</u> and Spukanee teams' progress. Elizabeth was out weeding her garden and busying herself with odd chores around the place that had accumulated while they were away. She figured this would be a good day to get all those kinds of tasks done with so much undivided time.

The noon meal was over and Lillian and Delbert were down for a nap. Hannah was pulling some weeds out of a portion of the garden her mother had sectioned off for her. She had planted some of her favorites: carrots, beans, corn, and beets. Elizabeth glanced up to the sound of a cluster of Spukanee families that were passing by, traveling north for spring fishing.

Elizabeth rose to greet them, wiping her hands on her apron. As they visited, Hannah peeked around the wild rose bushes that grew to the side of the garden. She watched children her age, noticing they were riding ponies about the size of Angel Spirit. Her eyes grew with excitement and her mind swarmed with plans.

She moved to the side and caught the attention of a couple little girls. They watched her with curious eyes. She waved to them. The girls glanced at each other and back at Hannah, who was smiling. The girls gave a slight wave in return. Hannah crept close, cautious of adult attention. She wanted to talk to the girls alone.

Hannah kept Elizabeth in view, but was almost crouching in hopes her mother wouldn't catch her movements out of the corner of her eye. She crept up in between the two girls and their ponies. She saw there were about six kids on horses near her age and gave them an inviting smile.

"Do you guys wanna come and see my horse?" Hannah pointed to the corral where Angel Spirit was poking her nose through the poles hoping to catch the scent of the other horses.

The girls glanced at one another and nodded. They followed Hannah over to the corral and dismounted. The tallest of the pair reached her hand out and let Angel Spirit smell her scent. She giggled as the pony's lips nibbled on her fingers. She snapped her hand back quickly. Hannah and the other girl giggled too. Not really speaking each other's language, they had to look, point, and laugh.

"Do you like him?" Hannah said in a very broken attempt at the Sinyekst tongue.

The two Spukanee girl's eyes grew wide. They nodded and answered in their language. Hannah cupped her pudgy hand over her mouth and gasped. *They understood me*, she thought.

The girls began to talk up a storm in their own Salish language, but Hannah stood shaking her head back and forth with her hands out in front of her face. "I don't really speak like you do," she tried to tell them. Hannah wiggled her hands back and forth, "No, no, no. I don't understand."

Finally the girls caught on, exchanged glances, and laughed. They giggled and nodded.

"Do you wanna race"—Hannah pointed from one pine tree that stood close by to another one several yards down the lane headed to Jack's place—"from there to there?"

Smiles sprouted on the Spukanee girls' faces. They nodded.

Hannah gestured to the others and eyed the girls. They turned, waving the other young kids over. Hannah peered in her mother's direction and saw her hands talking in circles with her back to them all. Elizabeth was plenty busy with her socializing and Hannah knew she loved to visit. She had no idea what her mother and the Spukanee people were talking about, but it must have been good because there was a lot of laughing and head nodding.

The other kids wandered over and the Spukanee girls' filled them in as they pointed to the starting tree and the one that they would pass to finish the race. The shorter girl caught the eye of an older one and motioned her over to be at the finishing tree to proclaim the winner.

Hannah rushed to tack up her pony. She was so thrilled, she struggled to get the latigo through the girth ring and knot it around to secure the saddle. Once the spitfire was able to settle her antsy nerves, she grabbed the bridle and slid the bit into the pony's mouth then slipped the headstall over her ears. She led Angel Spirit out to the mounting stump her father made for her and she climbed up and over the saddle, sitting big and tall upon her pony. She gave the sorrel-and-white a quick rub and then walked her in a few circles, just as she saw her auntie do.

The group watched her peculiar ways in silence. They neither chided her nor applauded. Hannah didn't care what she looked like to others, she knew the way her Auntie Spupaleena handled her horses made her win and that was all the reason she needed.

When Hannah was done, she trotted her pony over to the others and nodded. They all lined up and waited until the older girl was at the finish tree and had her hand in the air to give the signal to go. Hannah glanced over her shoulder to see that her mother was still deep in conversation. She smiled and turned her focus back to the older girl. Hannah gave Angel Spirit a reassuring pat and hung on tightly to the saddle horn.

Angel Spirit stood there, gawking at the horses next to her, seeming to wonder what they were all doing there. She whinnied and stomped her front hooves, shaking her head. Hannah began humming to the pony, willing the tiny beast to settle down and pay attention. Her tiny body shook with the thrill of eagerness.

Then in a matter of seconds, the start girl's arm dropped and seven ponies shot forward like an arrow out of a tight bow string.

Elizabeth screamed from the cracking noise of hoof on dirt and spun around. The others took off after them and stopped once they realized the kids were just having a friendly race. Elizabeth caught on about the same time pressing her hand to her stomach. She placed her face in her hands, thanking God nothing horrible was happening.

The Spukanee people sat on their horses and watched the race, searching for their child and cheering loudly.

Hannah could only hear the pounding of hoof beats. She was inches in the lead but felt like she was soaring feet above the rest of the children. All the little miniature racers ran in a tight pack and within minutes the race was over. Hannah reined her lively pony to a halt and circled her around, nearly bumping into those that pulled back to slow their ponies. For a moment she was elated, until the image of her mother's fuming face burst in her mind.

"Hannah," Elizabeth hollered.

The girl pretended to hear nothing.

"Hannah," Elizabeth waved and clapped her hands. Surprise melted into a broad smile. Hannah dropped her chin and eyed the ground.

"Hannah, why aren't you answering me?" Elizabeth placed her hands on her daughter's knee and rubbed it gently.

Tears pooled in the little girl's eyes and she sniffed, unable to say a word.

"Hannah, dear, it's all right. I'm not mad that you raced. In fact, I'm so happy that you won." Elizabeth leaned into her daughter, pulling her into a gentle hug.

"Really? You are, Mama?" Hannah wiped her tears away with her shirt sleeve and a smile blossomed on her round face.

"Oh, yes I am." Elizabeth nodded. "I'm so proud of you. I bet you can't wait to tell your Auntie Spuppy tomorrow when they return."

Hannah sat up straight. "I can't wait, Mama, I can't."

The others clapped and cheered and Hannah beamed with pride.

Elizabeth invited the group for some tea and corn bread before continuing on their journey. They gladly accepted. Hannah went to put Angel Spirit away. The other kids tied their ponies to surrounding trees and followed Hannah to the cabin. After an hour, the Spukanee families gathered their horses and set off. Elizabeth continued her chores, humming as she worked, while Hannah plunked down on her bed and drifted off to sleep.

The sun was setting by the time Phillip and the racers arrived back home. They were tired, hungry, and in need of a good scrubbing. Delbert squealed at the sight of his papa and Lillian smiled, kicked, and cooed. Hannah waited patiently to tell her father and auntie about the race. She wanted their full attention. Plus her mother made her promise to leave everyone alone while they put their horses up and unloaded their packs. She squirmed as though bugs danced inside her shirt.

Finally it was her turn and the little spitfire told her story as arms flailed, eyes danced, and legs stomped. A horse's whinny sounded a time or two as well.

Spupaleena's eyes danced as her protégé played out the scene. Pekam jabbed his sister often saying, "Just like you, <u>lth</u>kickha."

Everyone cheered when Hannah finished and she ran for her papa, leaping into his arms and receiving a rush of hugs and kisses. Delbert padded over to him and hugged his leg as he squealed in delight.

Once in bed for the night, the girl fell fast asleep and dreamt of girls, ponies, and the breeze tickling her chubby little face.

"I've never seen our daughter this excited." Elizabeth chuckled. She took a sip of her lukewarm tea and set it in her lap in a cuddling manner. "Poor thing acted like I was going to oust her from the saddle and send her to bed without supper."

Phillip smiled. "She is her auntie. I wish I had been here to see it."

"Next time."

"Yeah, I'm sure there will definitely be a next time." Phillip stood to bank the fire for the night. Tired from the last several days, he stumbled over to the logs and banked the fire, looking forward to a good night's sleep.

Chapter 20

Spupaleena was leading Dusty toward the staging area; she stopped, taking a moment to thank God for the beautiful day he had blessed her with to race in. She opened her eyes, squinting against the late morning sun and looked up on the northern hill of the Kettle Falls landscape to adore the carpet of wildflowers dancing in the breeze as though they were celebrating along with the spectators. Their brilliant hues settled her nerves until her focus was unexpectedly assaulted by the fool. She took a step back as her eyes locked on Hahoola<u>who</u>'s.

She stared at him with her mouth gaping. He peered at her with a look that expressed deep sorrow. He watched her as if he had something to say, but didn't know how to convey it. Spupaleena slammed her eyes shut for a moment and then reopened them slowly and looked up to see if it was just a dream or trick of the piercing sun. Her pulse raced and a blank look formed on her face.

Forgiveness is yours, Daughter.

Spupaleena jumped at the voice. She didn't know if it was in her mind or if Pekam had been standing beside her, he would have heard it as well. Spupaleena shifted her gaze from the ground back to the color-filled hill. He was gone. She searched in all directions, squinting against the sun and into the trees. She shaded her view with her hands. Nothing. He was gone. Was it a trick her mind had been playing on her? No. He was there. He looked different. Something must have occurred and he'd had a change of heart.

"God, I do forgive. I know sometimes I grab and take that forgiveness back and hang on for dear life, but I lay my hate, anger, and pride at you feet. Forgive me. Give me a heart filled with passion for you and your will for me. Wash away my insecurities and protect me from the tricks of the enemy…and Creator God, please watch over Hahoola<u>who</u> and his family."

"<u>Lth</u>kickha, what's going on?" Pekam gently laid a hand on her shoulder as he walked up and stood by his sister.

I saw him, again."

"Who?"

"The foo—Hahoola<u>who</u>. Something changed…he's different. I don't know…" Spupaleena's gaze was fixed on the hillside.

"Spupaleena we have a race. Come on, let's go and get ready." Pekam took hold of her wrist and began to lead her toward the horses.

She took a few steps, still searching the trees for one last glimpse. Forgiveness couldn't be that easy, could it? *Focus.* She turned and followed her brother. *Kewa, focus.*

I have a race to run. She shook her lingering thoughts away as Dusty stopped and jerked her mind back to reality. She stumbled and Pekam caught her.

"What's the matter with you?"

"Nothing"—Spupaleena righted herself and pulled away from Pekam—"just forgot I still had a grip on the lead rope."

Pekam tossed her an impatient look and walked off. "If you're serious about today, you can come on your own; I shouldn't have to hold your hand," he said, peering at her from over his shoulder.

The corners of Spupaleena's mouth turned up at her brother's brash words. She was grateful he loved her enough to speak the truth. She straightened her buckskin dress as a sudden flood of pink stained her face. She glanced around to see who was watching, gave a small smile, and scurried to catch up with Pekam. She was thankful most people weren't paying attention.

As Spupaleena walked, she imagined the perfect exchange in her mind as she fought off the butterflies taking flight in her stomach. She gulped in deep breaths and let them out slowly until her head felt light and then breathed normally. *Smooth, light, hop, hop, hop, lift, on, and run.* She repeated her plan over and over in her mind with exact visual effects.

Once Spupaleena was at Dusty's side, she crouched down and ran her palms over his legs and back. She felt no heat. Next she picked up each hoof and only a slight red shadow gave face to the bottom of his right hoof. Spupaleena gently let go of his leg and he set it down in the dirt.

"Time to pray," Ta <u>huh</u>t Skumhist said as she hurriedly walked up to Spupaleena. "Come on." Hun han neekun was on her heels and waved Spupaleena forward.

Spupaleena stood and followed the girls. They all circled up and laid their hands on horse and rider. Skumhist led the usual prayer of protection and wisdom. Once he finished, horses, handlers, and catchers rode off to their respective transition points.

Spupaleena looked up to see Simill<u>k</u>ameen watching her. The usual scowl sat unattended on her weathered and wrinkled face. Spupaleena smiled and nodded merely to humor herself. Simill<u>k</u>ameen's expression stayed the same. She wondered if the old lady ever did smile even as a young child.

Pekam and Spupaleena hopped on their mounts, all with saddles this time, and began to warm up their stallions. It wasn't long until the birdlike whistle sounded for the starters to line up—five teams in all.

"I got you this time, <u>lthk</u>ickha," Pekam teased.

"Not in this lifetime, sintahoos." Spupaleena smiled, but deep inside she knew it was possible for Dusty to come up lame in the race.

Spupaleena shut out the noise of the crowd from her mind and began to sing, "Ponies, beautiful ponies, running in the mountains so grateful to see, many colors the Creator formed us to be."

The shrill of the start cry pierced the hot, thick air and dirt flew to the pounding rhythm of hooves as the horses sped away. Rolling dust covered the spectators view, but they continued to cheer for their favored rider.

Up on the hill, somewhere in the center of the course, stood Hahoola<u>who</u> in the shadows of the fir trees. He smiled eagerly ready to watch and see who the winner would be. He was happy Ska ka ka and Pelpalwheechula were doing so well. They deserved it. He had watched them practice a few weeks ago from a distance and knew the team was working hard for the smooth transition and flawless timings. Someday he would ask his past teammates for their forgiveness as well.

The racers were approaching the first exchange, and it was one of the best the handlers and catchers had been a part of. They clapped and jumped up and down like little kids as the riders tore away with their fresh mount. Dusty had made it.

The upcoming jumps included three downed logs several feet apart that were dragged in specifically for this race. Spupaleena was in the lead only by a head's length. Pekam was right behind her, and the rest were all packed together. Noonwheena hit the first jump, took a few long strides and went for the second. He clipped the front of his foreleg on a jagged broken off branch still attached to the log and put a three inch gash in his foreleg. A five inch splinter hung out of the cut with bright red blood streaming down his leg.

Noonwheena began to falter and Spupaleena could feel him lose speed. She knew the stallion would rather come up lame then disappoint his owner. His heart was so big and he loved his job. The sorrel-and-white was born to run. Spupaleena made the split decision to rein him in. Winning a race was not more important than the health and wellbeing of her horses.

Pekam quickly past her as did the others. An expression of concern splashed across his face as he galloped by and caught his sister's attention. Spupaleena was on her knees, mouthing, "Go" as she waved him on. Pekam nodded and turned his focus on the upcoming transition. The remaining racers readied themselves for the last exchange and a couple more obstacles to overcome: running through a wide, shallow stream and finally taking a steep hill up and back down to the finish rope.

Once Noonwheena came down to a halt, Spupaleena dismounted and carefully pulled the long splinter out of his front leg. Blood flowed freely. She searched the area for something to stop the bleeding; her gaze landed on her feet. She tore off the legging of her moccasin and wrapped it around his wound, tying if off with the strip of leather that had been wound around the end of her braid. She winced at the pain in her knees and shoulder and rubbed her bloody hands in the grass. She dismissed her own bumps and bruises as they were only superficial and would deal with them after taking care of Noonwheena.

They limped back to the start line. Spupaleena felt a calm come over her knowing she had made the right decision. She held her head high figuring Pekam would shout out to Chy chy Pum Sn'e as to why his sister was not at the final exchange. She knew they would all understand and would have made the same call if they had been in her situation.

Pekam was now leading the pack. To everyone's surprise, the rider's transfers were impeccable, and they galloped off, leaving clouds of dust swirling in the air. The handlers of the last leg hollered even louder than the previous ones, and the escalating excitement spurred the riders on. The horses dug in as they all vied for the lead.

The stream would be an easy one with a sandy floor and soft, grassy approaches. All four horses whisked through the water with the speed and boldness of an otter, lunging up onto the foot-high bank that took them to a narrow incline. Pekam pulled his weight forward as his horse began to climb the steep, craggy hill hugging a rock wall. He rubbed the red roan's neck and shortened the rein preventing jerky lunges made by his anxious stud. He could hear the heavy, staccato breaths coming out of the horse's mouth that flanked him.

"Steady boy," Pekam said using a soothing tone. "We'll make it." He held the fast walking pace until they crested the hill and then Pekam let the roan have his head. A rush of energy kicked in and off they whirled down the slope and to the finish rope.

The horses ran in a tight pack as no one rider was ready to give up and throw in the towel. They jostled for position as the horses flew down the side of the knoll toward the finish rope that was a half mile away. It was around a bend and out of sight, but the horses could smell the humans and knew they were close. The animals willed themselves with a renewed strength that pumped through their veins. Sweat drenched their bodies, running down their legs.

Within minutes, the rope came into sight and the animals surged toward the braided horsehair rope. Thick veins protruded under the horses' skin as riders stretched their hands forward and tucked their chins. Pekam crossed the line with the others inches behind.

The braided rope ripped out of the holders' hands, tearing pieces of flesh as it cracked into the scorching air. The two men who had been holding the rope hopped up and down shouting Pekam's name. They felt no pain in the rush of exhilaration.

Pekam slowly reined the roan to a halt, turned, and headed back for the starting area. A smile graced his dirt-caked face exposing snow-white teeth. He lifted his arms into the air and let out an ear-piercing yell. The other riders were astonished to lose to such a young boy. Anger, frustration, and embarrassment crossed their paint streaked faces as some hung their heads. Yet in reality, shock was nowhere to be found as those left behind knew the name and reputation of Pekam's trainer.

On his way back, Pekam noticed a movement in the brush near the edge of the tree line. He glanced over searching for what he thought would be a whitetail deer. To his amazement, Hahoola<u>who</u> stepped out of the brush and nodded, lifting his arm in a congratulatory manner. Pekam nearly fell off his horse.

"She was telling the truth," he mumbled. And then Hahoola<u>who</u> was gone.

Simillkameen reluctantly helped Spupaleena clean and bandage Noonwheena's wound. She mumbled something about the brainless beasts as she worked. Glancing up, Spupaleena saw her father strolling toward her with several men at his side. He was smiling and nodding. As they got near, she could hear him talking about Dusty's exceptional qualities as well as Quiy Skets. Her heart raced, and her palms became wet and sticky.

Pekam and the other riders had not yet appeared; everyone waited anxiously. The teammates from the first legs started to straggle in, yet it would be a while for the others. Spupaleena didn't want to start any negotiations until her brother rode up. His chances of winning were high, but not guaranteed.

Simillkameen finished wrapping the stud's leg, grunted, and waddled off. Spupaleena smiled and shook her head. She called after the old lady, "Lim lumt, Simillkameen." The woman just kept walking. Spupaleena grinned and handed the bay Overo off to Kookyuma In-tee-tee-huh so he could go and stake the animal out. She washed her hands, wiping them on her doeskin dress and walked to face the men. She set her gaze on her father, waiting for him to finish and address her.

"Stumpkeelt, these men are interested in breeding their mares to your stallions. I have told them a little bit, but thought you would want to share the specifics."

He stood and smiled, stepping backward and allowing her to be a grown woman—the one in charge of her horse breeding operation.

Spupaleena nodded to her father, a gesture of respect and admiration. The horsemen noticed the manner in which father and daughter carried on. They exchanged glances and grinned. Spupaleena gestured to a soft grassy spot in the shade of some poplar trees edging a small stream. "Let's go get a cool drink and sit in the shade and talk."

The men agreed and followed. Spupaleena peered over her shoulder, searching for Pekam and the others who would be on their way back. Skumhist nodded. "They'll be here by the time our mouths are refreshed, and we can all meet, that is if I'm allowed to come and listen." He glanced down at his daughter, beaming with pride.

She smiled back. "I would love to have you come. Your wisdom and advice might come in handy, Mistum."

His chest swelled and he stood a bit taller. Father and daughter walked together, and for the first time, to visit with men about…horses. Spupaleena never thought this day would come. She said a little prayer of thanksgiving and asked for wisdom as they strolled along.

Cool, fresh water was consumed and a relative brought them a cedar basket full of fresh berries and smoked salmon. Spupaleena, Skumhist, and the men were just starting to dig in when a soft murmur of voices in the distance caught their attention. Spupaleena jumped up, scanning the area. She couldn't see anything. A roar of talk began to gather momentum and she stood on a nearby stump. Still nothing. She climbed on a taller boulder. Trees blocked her view.

Skumhist could no longer watch his daughter. "Go, we'll talk when you get back."

Spupaleena eyes pleaded with the waiting men. They smiled and waved her off, understanding her longing to see how Pekam had finished. Earlier the men had agreed to stay longer so they could all celebrate. There was plenty of time to make deals. They had traveled far and wished to get in on the festivities and dancing that would go into the early morning hours.

Cheering broke out and her pace hurried from a walk to a jog. Voices began to chant her brother's name causing her face to light up. Spupaleena's eyes darted from person to person as she scanned the crowd. The fringe of her doeskin dress swayed frantically to each step and goose bumps dotted her arms and the back of her neck. She couldn't reach him fast enough.

Soon the crowd parted and let her slip through to a waiting Pekam, who sat gleaming yet humble on his stallion that was caked in dried, stiff sweat. The other three racers stood behind him and began to clap. The onlookers wore astonished expressions, but quickly softened them with grins and joined in. Skumhist was soon by his daughter's side and hugged her tightly. They joined in the celebration by making high-pitched birdlike sounds.

Pekam peered down at his family, pointing a single finger in the air, directed to the heavens. He slid off his horse and made his way to his family. Skumhist let go of his daughter and she turned to face her brother. Pride poured out of her like a rushing stream cascading over a waterfall. "You should have won that race. I wouldn't have if Noonwheena hadn't gotten hurt." He placed his broad hands on her strong shoulders.

Spupaleena shook her head. "Loot, sintahoos. You've worked hard and I'm so happy for this win of yours." She grinned through joyous tears, hugging him tightly.

Pekam let go of her. "But you—"

Spupaleena put a finger to his lips. "Loot. Praise God and enjoy this moment. Once I'm back on…" She winked up at her younger brother who stood inches taller than she and growing rapidly. They grabbed one another and jumped around foolishly.

Simillkameen elbowed her way to the front of the crowd. Boisterous cheering trickled down to a faint buzz making the pairs of feet come to a halt. The siblings parted and turned their attention to her; astounded that the old, bitter woman was facing them. She glanced at Pekam, shifted her gaze to the three boys suddenly looking whipped, slouching on their horses, and back again to Pekam. Ska ka ka's face turned red. The corners of her cranky mouth began to turn up—slightly.

Spupaleena jerked her gaze to her brother and they smiled at one another, stifling laughs that begged to escape. They looked back at the squatty woman unsure how they should respond. Her wrinkled eyes sparkled and she began to chuckle. That chuckle rapidly turned into a belly jerking laugh that caused tears to pool in her eyes. She bent over from laughing so hard, pressing her hand to her stomach.

Pekam and Spupaleena stood, watching the woman, wondering if she would remain on her feet she was so giddy. Having never witnessed this burst of amusement, they were somewhat bewildered. Skumhist's shoulders danced as he glanced from his children to the aged healer and soon he too was laughing. The crowd chimed in as a quiet chuckle swelled into an outright roar.

This was a moment in time that would be talked about for generations. The day the adolescent Sinyekst boy triumphed over his legendary sister…and how the old, cranky woman decided to smile.

Pekam took hold of his sister's hand in one of his and his father's hand in the other. They walked off together to reminisce about the day's event and to plan and dream about the next stage of their lives—together.

Painted Ponies

By Carmen Peone

Baby girl, baby girl, what do you see?
A red pony
A white pony
A brown pony
Kewa, three.
Running in the field so happy and free,
A black pony
A blue pony
A green pony
Kewa, three.
Come and ride me,
I will take you places
And we will see many sites,
Please, baby girl, come to me.
Baby girl, baby girl, tell me
What do you see?
An orange pony
A yellow pony
A purple pony,

Kewa, three.
Ponies, beautiful ponies
Running in the mountains
So grateful to see
Many colors the Creator
Formed us to be.

Arrow Lakes Word Index

Note: <u>K</u> sounds like the regular *k*, but in the back of the throat, a guttural sound. <u>Lth</u> sound is made by placing the tongue up against the back of the upper front teeth and blowing.

Chapter One

Word *Meaning*
Pronunciation/Sounds like
Spupaleena *Rabbit*
Spup-a-leena (like Tina)
Pekam *Bobcat*
Pe (sounds like Pea)- kam (rhymes with Sam)
Sinyekst *Speckled Fish, or Bull Trout, People*
Sin-ye (yie rhymes with lie)-kst
Hahoola<u>who</u> *Rattlesnake*
Ha (hah)- hoola- <u>who</u> (soft blowing sound)
Kewa *Yes*
Ke (key)- wa (wah, rhymes with jaw)
Sintahoos *Brother*

Sin- ta (taw)- hoos (rhymes with loose)
Mistum *Father*
Mist- um
Skumhist *Black Bear*
Skum (scum)- hist (rhymes with beast)
Kook̲yuma In-tee-tee-huh *Little Salmon*
K̲ (back of throat)- oo- k̲-yuma (you)- ma (mah)
In-tea-tea-huh (key)
Seech Sneewt *New Wind*
Sea ch (see key) S- new-t
Simillk̲ameen *Swan*
Si-milk̲-a-meen (sounds like mean)
Hun han neekun *Bug*
Hun (hon as is *hon*ey)- han (haughn)- neek-un
Ta huht Skumhist *Sugarbear*
tah-huh (key)-t- skum (scum)- hist (rhymes with beast)
Toom *Mother*
Too-m

Chapter Two

Loot *No*
Loo (Lou)- t
Ska ka ka *Chicken*
Skah- kah- kah
Toople *Spider*
Too-p-l (e is silent)
Impee eels T-san *Happy Grasshopper*
Imp-ee eels t-san (sawn)

Quiy Ha-hau *Black Crow*
Qu- iy (eye) hau-hau

Chapter Three

Chy chy pum Sn'e *Screaming Elk*
Chi (rhymes with eye)- chi- pum (rhymes with come) sn'e (rhymes with knee)
Kookyuma Yaw Yat *Tiny but Strong*
K (back of throat)- oo- k-yuma (you)- ma (mah) yow- yat (like yawt)
Quill Say Ups (Pia) *Red Tail Hawk*
Quil- say- you-ps (Pea-uh)
Kelowna *White Grizzly*
Key-low-nuh
Seelwha Sn'e *Big Elk*
Seal-whah Sn'e (rhymes with knee)
Pelpalwheechula *Butterfly*
Pel (rhymes with bell)- pal- wheech (rhymes with beach)- u (you)- la (luh)
Swas Kee *Blue Jay*
Swah-s- key
Quiy Sket *Black Rain*
Qu- iy (eye)- Sket (like jet, the k–back of throat)

Chapter Four

Mistum *Father*
Mist- um

Lim Lumt *Thank You*
Lim (rhymes with Tim)- lumt
Wi *Yes*
Like why but the "y" is cut short

Chapter Five

Lthkickha *Older Sister*
<u>Lth</u> (see sound guide)- kick- ha (rhymes with ma)
Squasee *Son*
Squa-see

Chapter Six

Noonwheena *Believer*
Noon-whe (rhymes with tea)- nah
Spaoos Newt *Heart Breaker*
Spah-oos new-t

Chapter Seven

Naux *One*
Nah-x

Chapter Eight

Sinyekst *Arrow Lakes (Speckled fish or Bull Trout)*
Sin-i (like eye)-kst

Stumpkeelt *Daughter*
Stump- k (back of throat)- eelt

Chapter Nine

Incheechun *Wolf*
In-ch (sound guide)-ee-ch-un
N haneekin *Beetle*
n- han (rhymes with con) neekin
Stoonhuh *Beaver*
Stoon-huh (sound guide)
Chy-ha *Crawdad*
Ch- i (like eye)- ha (haw)
Sinkaleep *Coyote*
Sin-ka (kaw)- leep
Cheelkst Kawup *Five Horses*
Ch (sound guide)- ee-lkst ka (kaw)- up
Swa *Cougar*
Sw-aw (like saw)
Wha Welwho *Fox*
Whah- whale-who (soft blowing sound)
Spokalitz *Ling*
Spoke-a-litz (like glitz)

Chapter Ten

Naux *One*
Naw-x
Aseel *Two*

U (like mud)-seal
Kalthese *Three*
Ka (like cat)- lth (sound guide) ee-s

Chapter Eleven

Oo pa Weekin *Stink Bug*
oo- pa (paw)-wee-kin

Chapter Twelve

Nee Ap Kukneeya *Forever Listening*
Knee- ap (like nap) K (back of throat)- u (as in m*u*d)- k (back of throat)
nee (like knee)- ya (yaw)

Chapter Fourteen

Spukanee *Spokane*
Spuck-uh-knee
Kalispeliwho *Kalispel*
Cal-i-spell-ee-who (soft blowing sound)
Tuklthmeelwho *Woman*
Tuck-lth (sound guide)- meel (meal)- who (soft blowing sound)

Chapter Fifteen

K̲ook̲yuma May Ooya *Tiny Racoon*
K̲ (back of throat)- oo- k̲-yuma (you)- ma (mah)
May-oo-ya (yah)